NO DEFENSE

Janine knew she should not have come to this secluded spot with Lord Mark Talbot. She should not have listened to his words of adoration, but instead ended his hopes of winning her heart at once. Above all, she should not have let his lips touch hers, even for an instant.

Now as she saw the furious face of Richard Stuart gazing down at Mark and her with harsh accusation in his eyes, Janine searched for words of explanation—and found none.

It was Mark Talbot who rose to her defense—as he challenged Richard Stuart to a duel.

How could Janine stop her folly from costing either the life of the man she wished she could love—or the life of the man she wished she did not . . . ?

The Unwilling Heiress

Ⓞ SIGNET REGENCY ROMANCE   (0451)

Amorous Escapades

☐	THE UNRULY BRIDE by Vanessa Gray.	(134060—$2.50)
☐	THE DUKE'S MESSENGER by Vanessa Gray.	(138856—$2.50)
☐	THE DUTIFUL DAUGHTER by Vanessa Gray.	(090179—$1.75)
☐	THE RECKLESS GAMBLER by Vanessa Gray.	(137647—$2.50)
☐	THE ABANDONED BRIDE by Edith Layton.	(135652—$2.50)
☐	THE DISDAINFUL MARQUIS by Edith Layton.	(145879—$2.50)
☐	FALSE ANGEL by Edith Layton.	(138562—$2.50)
☐	THE INDIAN MAIDEN by Edith Layton.	(143019—$2.50)
☐	RED JACK'S DAUGHTER by Edith Layton.	(144880—$2.50)
☐	LADY OF SPIRIT by Edith Layton.	(145178—$2.50)
☐	THE NOBLE IMPOSTER by Mollie Ashton.	(129156—$2.25)
☐	LORD CALIBAN by Ellen Fitzgerald.	(134761—$2.50)
☐	A NOVEL ALLIANCE by Ellen Fitzgerald.	(132742—$2.50)
☐	THE IRISH HEIRESS by Ellen Fitzgerald.	(136594—$2.50)
☐	ROGUE'S BRIDE by Ellen Fitzgerald.	(140435—$2.50)

Prices slightly higher in Canada.

Buy them at your local bookstore or use this convenient coupon for ordering.

NEW AMERICAN LIBRARY,
P.O. Box 999, Bergenfield, New Jersey 07621

Please send me the books I have checked above. I am enclosing $_____
(please add $1.00 to this order to cover postage and handling). Send check
or money order—no cash or C.O.D.'s. Prices and numbers are subject to change
without notice.

Name_____

Address_____

City_____State_____Zip Code_____

Allow 4-6 weeks for delivery.
This offer is subject to withdrawal without notice.

The Unwilling Heiress

by
Sandra Heath

A SIGNET BOOK

NEW AMERICAN LIBRARY

SIGNET TRADEMARK REG. U.S. PAT. OFF. AND FOREIGN COUNTRIES
REGISTERED TRADEMARK—MARCA REGISTRADA
HECHO EN CHICAGO, U.S.A.

SIGNET, SIGNET CLASSIC, MENTOR, ONYX, PLUME, MERIDIAN AND
NAL BOOKS are published by New American Library,
1633 Broadway, New York, New York 10019

First Printing, May, 1981

3   4   5   6   7   8   9   10   11

PRINTED IN THE UNITED STATES OF AMERICA

PUBLISHER'S NOTE

The Unwilling Heiress

Chapter 1

The post-chaise clattered to a standstill on the wet cobbles behind the theater. There was still rain in the dark summer night, the tiny drops picked out by the weak lamps at the front of the battered old chariot.

A girl in blue dimity climbed wearily down with two bags, setting them down as she searched in her reticule for some coins to pay the post-boy. It was eleven o'clock, and suddenly the London night was alive with church bells chiming the hour. The two horses shifted and the boy growled at them.

"Want change?" he demanded of the girl, in a way surely calculated to intimidate.

His ploy was successful. Janine shook her head and picked up the bags again, walking slowly over the cobbles to the stage door. Dimly through the night, as the bells ended, she could hear the sound of the audience cheering and shouting inside. Strains of well-loved tunes drifted in the air. Peg Oldfield's songs, the most popular, most whistled, most hummed songs in London. Smiling fondly, Janine reached out to the bell-pull.

The doorman peered cautiously round the door, and

his stern face broke into a grin as he undid the various chains which protected the theater from any unwelcome intruders. "Miss Oldfield! Miss Jan! Oh, come in, come in out of the rain!" He seized the bags and took them inside, setting them down and looking out suspiciously into the night again before closing the door and putting the chains back, locking each one.

"It's like getting into the Tower of London!" Janine laughed, untying her straw bonnet and shaking her black hair.

"Getting in to see Peg Oldfield is as rewarding as getting into the treasure house itself." Dickon's bald head gleamed in the light of an old oil lamp as he looked at her. "My, my, you're a picture, a proper picture. What brings you back to us after all this time, eh?"

She looked at him in surprise. "Didn't you expect me, then? My mother sent for me."

"Reckon she wanted to surprise us all, eh? Well, turn round, then, let's take a look at you."

She turned obediently, and he looked her up and down, from her dainty calfskin shoes to her elegantly curled hair in its fashionable tumbles.

Then he nodded. "A proper young lady, and that's a fact. That there academy in Bath turned you out a treat, right enough."

"Miss Tarrant's Academy for Young Ladies." Janine pulled a face. "It was more fun back here in London."

He picked up the bags again, bending his head beneath the artificial archway used on stage sometimes, and Janine followed him. The atmosphere of the theater was permeating her already, as always it had done. Miss Tarrant had perhaps made a lady of Peg Oldfield's daughter, but beneath the surface, the theater was all she craved.

Dickon opened the dressing-room door and put the

bags down again. "She'll be a while yet, the show's only just started."

"I'll be all right here, Dickon."

He paused in the doorway again, smiling fondly at her. "Reckon there'll be a celebration later, eh? A welcoming for you?"

"I hope so."

He rubbed a finger against his nose and winked. "I'll *see* to it!"

She smiled as he closed the door, and then she looked around. It was a small room, lit by a single oil lamp on a table in the corner. Old posters decorated the walls, and countless costumes had been hung on hooks everywhere. A battered red velvet sofa stood to one side, some tissue paper scattered over it and a new gown tossed casually over its back had obviously just come from the dressmaker's. The dressing table was littered with pots and jars, and several wigs rested on pegs above it. There was a smell of smoke and perfume in the close air. Janine looked at the sofa again, remembering the countless times as a child that she had curled up there, watching her mother preparing for a show, or maybe sleeping there waiting to be taken home afterward in Peg Oldfield's notorious crimson and gold carriage. Everything about Peg Oldfield was notorious.

Janine's pale blue reflection shimmered in the mirror on the dressing table, and she picked up the oil lamp and went closer, setting the lamp down close to the mirror and then sitting on the stool to look at herself. The lamp light swayed for a while, a stream of smoke rising from the bright glass, but then as it steadied she could see herself clearly. She was like her mother in so many ways, with the same raven black hair, the same small, neat nose and the same clear complexion. But her mouth was not as wide and expressive—it would need a great deal of rouge to show up clearly on the stage— She looked at her eyes, so large and of such a dark blue they seemed almost violet. Perhaps her eyes were her finest point, she decided critically, widening them for a moment to study the effect. There was a flash of fire there, it was true, but was there enough to beguile an audience, to hold it spellbound throughout a show as Peg's did? Janine sighed.

The audience roared and stamped its feet with approval, and the sounds vibrated through the theater, drowning the faint drift of music for a moment. A tingle coursed through her body, stirring her as always it did. This time, this time she *had* to persuade her mother to change her mind. When Peg Oldfield gave up the stage, her daughter should be there to step into her shoes—

Janine studied her reflection again. One day the name of Janine Oldfield would be as great as her mother's. One of Peg's best-loved songs came clearly as the noise died away, and Janine mimed it, still watching her reflection. There should be a certain tilt of the head just there, but somehow she couldn't capture the essence of it. But it would come, it *would* come!

The jars of makeup were a clutter on the powdery surface of the dressing table, some of them open. It was the usual untidy mess Peg always left in her wake. Janine looked around at the delicate costumes hanging ŏn their hooks, each one with sequins, ribbons and flounces. And daring necklines. The colors and materials were rich and magnificent. Beside them hung the men's clothes for which Peg Oldfield was perhaps most famous. Janine smiled as she looked at the admiral's uniform. What would Lord Nelson have to say if he returned to see himself portrayed on stage by a beautiful actress with long legs and a tiny waist, and her hat at a saucy angle? Maybe he would have approved—

She twisted off the lid of a porcelain dish and dipped

her fingertips in the smooth rouge it contained. It had a smell and a texture all its own, not even vaguely like the Portuguese rouge permitted at Miss Tarrant's Academy. Slowly she applied it to her cheeks, smoothing it in and delighting in the feel of the creamy salve. But if she were preparing to go on stage, then the rouge would be applied more liberally— Janine dipped her fingers in again and applied some more, wiping her red-stained fingers on a cloth which already bore the marks of varying colors, ranging from black and gray to crimson and vermilion. Then she put smudges of violet above her eyes and emphasized them with dark thick lines as she had seen her mother do. When she sat back to study the effect she thought fleetingly that she had managed to make herself look more like a streetwalker than, say—Columbine? Her glance went to the dainty gown of white gauze with its garlands of pink and white roses. Getting up she lifted the flounced gown down, holding it against her body. But it was impossible to tell the effect with the thick blue dimity already there. Returning the gown to its hook she unbuttoned her pelisse and loosened the drawstring of her gown.

The gauze clung to her as if alive, its wired bodice feeling strange for a moment. How full the gown was, and how tight the waist—not at all like the fashion of the moment. She twirled and posed, watching her reflection. Perhaps she had been a little heavy-handed with her eyes; she looked as if she had fisticuffed with Gentleman Jackson himself! Suddenly the door opened, and she turned with a gasp, relaxing as she saw that it was only her mother's dresser, Dobby.

"Oh, Dobby, you gave me a start!"

Dobby's eyes went over her for a moment, and then she set down the costume she had been carrying, folding her hands neatly before her black silk dress. "And well you might look guilty, Miss Jan! You'd best get out of that before your mother comes off stage."

"Oh, Dobby, she'll be a while yet. Besides, she will have to face the fact that I intend following in her footsteps."

Dobby looked away for a moment, picking up the costume and hanging it carefully on a hook. Her spectacles were perched on the end of her nose, and that, together with her long, thin nose made all the more prominent by her tightly pulled-back gray hair, made her look like some great black bird. She looked at Janine again. "It would still be better if you got out of that lot right now. It may be that she won't be on stage for her full show, it's not often that she is these days."

Janine looked quickly at her. "What do you mean?"

"She ent well, Miss Jan, she ent well at all. To tell the honest truth, that's why I sent for you."

"*You* sent for me? I thought—"

"Well, I didn't want to frighten you none. She won't let on as she's ill, Miss Jan, not to me nor even to herself. But there's more an' more times of late when she can't go on at all, and if'n she does, then it ent for the whole show."

Janine stared at her. "But when—when I last saw her a month or so ago she seemed so well!"

"That were one of her better times, and that were why she went to Bath to see you then. She don't want you to worry none, but I reckon 'tis time she were made to face up to it."

There was something so very final and hopeless in the dresser's voice that Janine sat down suddenly on the old stool. "Dobby," she whispered in a frightened voice, "what are you telling me?"

Dobby blinked back the tears and took the girl's shaking hands. "Sweetheart, you mustn't reckon on Peg Oldfield being around for too much longer."

"Oh, no! No!"

Dobby's fingers tightened gently. "You mustn't let on as you've been told anything now—promise me?"

Janine looked up into the dresser's kindly, concerned face. "I promise."

"That's a good girl. Now then, let's get you out of this before she comes and catches you."

"Dobby, I meant what I said earlier. I want to be like my mother, to be as famous as she is if I can."

"Peg Oldfield didn't pay good money to send you to that there academy, having you taught to read and write proper, to speak French and such like, just to have you tripping on the stage. 'Tis as a *lady* she wants you to live, not as a actress."

"I'm Peg Oldfield's daughter, Dobby—not a lady."

Dobby straightened. "Peg's more of a lady than most people will ever know, Miss Jan. You don't know the half of it, not the half of it."

Janine stood to let the dresser help her out of the gown. They were suddenly quiet, for there seemed nothing suitable to say. Beyond the room the sounds of the theater went on, with the chattering, laughing chorus as they hurried up to the stage from their large dressing room nearby, and the deafening cheers of the audience as Peg Oldfield sang her most famous song. *When I grow up, I'll go to sea; a jolly jack tar, that'll be me*— Janine closed her eyes, imagining Peg in her tight, patched trousers striding across the bright stage, her striped jacket revealing a decidedly feminine shape, a cheeky lock of black hair tumbling from beneath her hat—

Dobby gasped suddenly. "That's her last song, she's brought it forward! Oh, my Lord, she mustn't catch you with all that stuff on your face."

Janine picked up the stained cloth again and began to wipe the makeup off, and Dobby moaned. "Lord above, you didn't put it on without that there oil, did you? We'll *never* get it all off quick now!"

"Oh, Dobby!" Feverishly Janine continued wiping, but the smears of violet, black and red made her look like the picture of a North American Indian she had seen once.

The final cheers began, and with them the thump-thump of the audience's feet as they called Peg back again. But she didn't return, for in a moment she was opening the dressing-room door.

Her presence filled the room as she stood there, her hands on her hips, eyeing Janine as she hastily buttoned her pelisse. The magnificent dark blue eyes came to rest on her daughter's stained face. Without a word she strode to the dressing table and picked up a bottle of clear oil, pushing it into Janine's hand. "Wipe it off with this," she said shortly.

Dobby cleared her throat. "A drink, Miss Peg?"

Peg nodded wearily. "Something good and strong, if you please, Dobby."

"But—"

"No buts, not tonight; just do as I ask."

Dobby's eyes met Janine's in the mirror, and then the dresser went to a cupboard and took out a bottle of cognac. Peg poured herself a very liberal glass and drank it in two gulps, pausing with her eyes closed as the fiery spirit made its way down her throat. Then she looked at Janine again.

"If I ever see you with that paint on your face again, missy, I'll tan you to within an inch of you life, is that clear?"

"Yes, Mama." Janine bit back the anger and frustration.

Peg smiled suddenly, her face lighting up. "It's good to see you again, sweetheart, but why have you come? Why didn't you let me know?"

"I—I wanted to surprise you. Miss Tarrant's Academy has closed for a while—er, measles."

"Measles? Good heavens! So, you've come to stay with me for a while?"

"Yes."

"I shall love having you." Peg sat down and began to remove the makeup she had so skillfully applied, and Janine watched her. It had been six weeks since last she had seen her mother, but the change was marked. She had lost weight so that the trousers which originally had been skin-tight were now loose. There were shadows beneath her eyes which were revealed by the removal of the makeup, and there was no sparkle in the beautiful smile as she caught Janine's eyes. "A sorry sight, eh?"

Janine said nothing.

Peg put down the cloth and turned on the stool to look at her daughter. "I've been feeling a little under the weather. Plays havoc with your looks."

"You're still the most beautiful woman in London."

"Ah, the most beautiful on the London stage maybe. Do you know, I was invited secretly to Carlton House last week. *Secretly!* Peg Oldfield goes nowhere secretly, not even on an assignation with the Prince Regent! I sent a very to-the-point note, I can tell you!"

Janine smiled, slipping her arms around her mother's shoulders and resting her head against the dark, smooth hair. "I'd like to have been a fly on the royal wall when he received that note!"

"No one, but *no one* commands Peg Oldfield anywhere."

Janine straightened. "Except Lord Wolfe?"

Peg breathed in slowly. "Janine, that is none of your concern."

"He's very notorious, Mama."

"A fitting partner for Peg Oldfield, then, don't you think?"

"He's gambled away his entire fortune, everyone knows that he has."

"And now he's gambling mine away too? Is that what you're on the verge of suggesting? Look, sweetheart, I don't want to quarrel with you, not on your first night in London."

"When are you seeing him again?"

"Tonight."

"Oh."

"Don't say it like that, for I'm very fond of David. Very fond."

There was a tremble in her voice and Janine touched her cheek quickly. "I'm sorry, Mama, truly I am, I didn't mean to upset you—"

"I know, sweetheart, I know. I just wish—well, I wish that you and David got on a little more, that's all."

"If he were to make an honest woman of you, I'd think more of him."

"I've been an honest woman once and that was taste enough for me. Now, where's my pink muslin?"

"Here," said Dobby who had been waiting patiently and silently by the dressing table.

Dickon knocked at the door. "His lordship's here, Miss Peg."

Chapter 2

Peg smoothed the pink muslin carefully, turning to inspect her profile in the mirror. When at last satisfied with her appearance, she called to Dickon. "Show his lordship in, Dickon, if you please."

David, Lord Wolfe, took off his shining top hat, smiling slowly at Peg, his lazy eyes moving warmly over her. "More beautiful than ever, my dearest Peg," he said softly, putting his hands to her waist and kissing her on the mouth.

Janine watched him with loathing. With his romantic dark hair and almost French looks, he was undoubtedly handsome. He dressed in the very latest fashions, a true Corinthian, flicking his handkerchief at imaginary specks of dust, and raising his fob-glass to inspect everything. Beau Brummel had been slightly better dressed, but there was surely no one else in the realm as cool, arrogant and supremely confident as this man. He was somewhere in his middle thirties, Janine guessed, but as slender and youthful as a boy of eighteen, and with his charm and boyish smile he played upon Peg's weaknesses as skillfully as the Biblical David had probably played his harp.

He turned suddenly as he saw Janine in the mirror. "Well, now, what a pleasant surprise." He caught her hand and raised it to his lips, lingering far more than was necessary over kissing it. He smelled of musk—or maybe civet cat, as Dobby had been heard more than once muttering under her breath! "How very charming you look, Janine."

"How kind of you to say so, my lord." Janine met his eyes coolly, determining never to address him by his first name as he had often suggested she do in the past.

Peg flushed a little, reaching to pick up her white fur mantle. "Well, now," she said brightly, "as we are journeying in your landau, David, then Janine may take my barouche to go home."

"Will you not dine with us, Janine?" he asked, his eyes resting on the *décolletage* of her dimity gown.

"No, thank you, for I think Dickon is arranging a little celebration for me."

"Oh." Peg bit her lip. "I hadn't thought—"

"It doesn't matter, Mama. You were hardly to know I was thinking of coming back tonight." Janine squeezed her mother's hands reassuringly.

"Yes, but I should be there, they'll think badly of me—"

"Nonsense. You go on and enjoy yourself, Dobby can have place of honor next to me, can't you Dobby?"

"That I can." Dobby smiled as she hung away the sailor costume.

"Perhaps David and I could—"

"No," said Janine almost too quickly, "you have your own plans and you must go ahead with them. Honestly, I shall not mind a bit." Nothing would make her spend an evening with Lord Wolfe and his hot eyes and damp hands! *Nothing!* Not even her mother's company!

Peg kissed her cheek swiftly and then was gone in a

haze of pink muslin and white fur. David picked up his hat and cane, pausing to look at Janine for a moment, his eyes dark. "What a liberated young lady you are, to be sure," he murmured, "even for 1806. Good night, Janine."

"Good night, my lord."

He smiled faintly, tapping on his hat, and then he walked out, closing the door behind him.

Dobby sighed with relief. "Lord above, what a toad that man is."

"Ah, but an aristocratic one." Janine smiled. Her smile faded. "I keep hoping that one day she'll see the light, that he's leeching from her as surely as any black-slimed worm."

"What a pleasant thought," said Dobby dryly. "Anyway, she's happy enough, and that's all that really matters, isn't it?"

Janine looked at the dresser. "I suppose so. Oh, Dobby, she doesn't look at all well."

"I know. Maybe, when you're alone with her late tonight, or tomorrow—any time—you can persuade her to rest more. Fewer performances, *far* fewer late nights—"

"She won't listen to me. She never has and I don't suppose she's about to change the habit of a lifetime."

Dobby smoothed her apron nervously. "She'd listen to the Toad."

"You ask him to speak to her then!"

Dobby glanced slyly at her. "He don't even know I exist. He knows you do, though."

"You mean he knows the low neckline of my gown exists!"

"That's hardly the way for a young lady to speak!"

"He makes me feel very unladylike."

"You could ask him, though, Miss Jan, he'd listen to you. He's about the only one to make her see sense."

"If he wants her to see sense. If she rests more and

gives fewer performances, Dobby, then there will be less money for him to fritter away."

Dobby sighed. "Well, if she won't listen to you, then someone will have to try him."

"Meaning me."

"Yes."

"You are an awful taskmaster at times, Dobby, far worse than Miss Tarrant! Very well, if Mama will not listen to me, then I give my word I will speak with His Odious Lordship."

Dobby beamed. "Now then, Dickon's fixed us up a fine big table at Cane's Tea Rooms down the road. We can have us some junketings, eh?"

"Cane's Tea Rooms? How very superior!"

"We're all allowed in on account of the nobs who come there only come to see the likes of us! I keep thinking I ought to spit, scratch and swear like an infantryman."

"To give the place some color, I presume?"

"That's correct. Honestly, the way those lorgnettes and so on are raised, like we was a flea circus!"

Janine laughed. "Oh, Dobby!"

"Come on then, I could sink my teeth in a few buns and some of that good Formosa they give us there. Hurry up, I'm *starving!*"

The long tables had been set together to accommodate the whole company, and their corner of the fashionable tea rooms was easily the most noisy, rowdy in the whole place, drowning the strains of music from the string quartet in their periwigs and coats of red and gold. The chandeliers high above glittered as the heat of the room moved the crystal droplets. Dark red silk covered the walls. The intimate tables were candlelit and each was curtained off discreetly. As Janine looked around she wondered how many illicit assignations were taking place in those darkened, secret places.

But the theater party was intent upon enjoying itself, and Janine had already come to the conclusion that the decidedly odd taste in her tea was something of an extremely potent alcoholic nature. She felt warm and relaxed, laughing at the jokes and listening to the reminiscences of some of the older members of the party. Great names of the past flowed over the tables, memories of famous plays, wondrous royal occasions and the dazzling concert put on in memory of Lord Nelson. She looked around at the laughing, smiling faces. Maybe they weren't genteel, maybe they were downright crude at times, but Janine felt far more at home with them than with the other young ladies at the academy. These were real people, people whose lives did not revolve around elaborate manners and society rituals.

She sipped the "tea" thoughtfully. No one had mentioned her mother's absence, or her obvious ill health; it was as if by some tacit agreement nothing would be said to mar the evening.

"Excuse me—"

A male voice spoke close by and Janine looked up with a start. A gentleman in black velvet and crisp white shirt sketched an elegant bow. "Your servant, ma'am."

"Sir?"

He was young and his face had a good-natured expression. He smiled easily and it was a genuine smile. "You so resemble Peg Oldfield, ma'am, that we—my friends are over there—we thought you must be related. To tell the truth, there's a handsome wager resting on the outcome of my next question."

"Next question, Mr.—?"

"Westenhaugh. Hal Westenhaugh. Yes, d'you see, we *know* in our hearts that you *are* related to the Wondrous Peg, and the fact that you're here with these good—er, people, suggests that you too must be in the theater."

Janine glanced at Dobby who was frowning very pointedly at her. "So, you have decided—what is your next question?"

"Miss Jan," muttered Dobby anxiously, "you *shouldn't!*"

Westenhaugh cleared his throat, toying with his fob seals. "Well, if we were to give you a list of four songs, which one would you stand up and sing for us?"

"Us?"

He indicated a table in a corner where three gentlemen sat with a pile of banknotes in front of them.

Dobby leaned closer. "Don't go any further, Miss Jan, your mother wouldn't—"

"Mother?" Westenhaugh leaned one elegant hand on the table next to Janine. "Damme, you're Peg Oldfield's *daughter?*" The last three words were said so loudly that the whole tea room seemed to become suddenly quiet. Everyone looked toward Janine.

"Yes, Mr. Westenhaugh," she said softly, "I am Peg Oldfield's daughter."

"And all set to step into her shoes! Well, blow me down with a feather! Another Oldfield as Glorious as the first." He bowed more deeply and Janine laughed.

"Oh, Vision," he said, bending to one knee, hands clasped in supplication toward her, "choose a ditty for us and bless our humble ears with your Divine voice!"

"Miss Jan!" hissed Dobby, sensing that Janine was enjoying the moment and might indeed choose and sing the song.

Janine was indeed enjoying the entertaining antics of Mr. Westenhaugh, and the relaxing influence of the well-laced tea made her reckless. Being adored and famous was her dream, and tonight, just for a little while, her dream was coming true.

"Let me see your list, Mr. Westenhaugh."

He took a slip of paper from his waistcoat pocket and handed it to her, glancing back triumphantly at his friends. Janine surveyed the four song titles, all of them popular favorites her mother had made famous.

"Don't, Miss Jan," said Dobby again.

"Oh, Dobby, what possible harm can it do? I'll sing this one, Mr. Westenhaugh."

"'When I grow up, a sailor I'll be'? Damme, I win! You will sing it, I mean, you won't change your mind, Miss Oldfield?" He looked anxiously at her, lowering his voice. "I still don't win the wager unless you sing the dratted thing as well."

"That dratted thing, sir, is one of my mother's songs and I'll thank you not to be so slighting when you speak of it!"

He looked contrite. "Forgive me, I mean no—er, insult. You will sing for us?"

"If, sir, you play the piano to accompany me."

"Me? God above, I ain't played a note since childhood!"

"Back in the mists of time?"

He smiled. "Not that far back, I suppose. Very well, I'll play, but you'll have to put up with less than genius, I fear."

The whole tea room clapped and cheered as Janine ignored Dobby's last-minute plea and got up. Everyone crowded around the piano as Mr. Westenhaugh flexed his fingers dramatically and played a few exercises to the mirth of all who detected the various bad notes.

Suddenly Dobby pushed her way through the crowds, tapping him on the shoulder. "Sir, you'll 'ave to step aside, I'll not have Peg's good song ruined by the likes of you. I'll play and do the song and Miss Jan justice."

Janine smiled at her, and a moment later the first trills of the well-known tune rippled expertly from Dobby's fingers. Janine struck a pose as her mother

did, and began to sing, twisting and turning as she
swaggered around the small space the crowd left for
her, catching up her skirts to reveal her dainty ankles.
She put everything into the song, imaginging she was
on the stage herself, and the imagining was so real that
she could almost feel the warmth of the oil lamps and
smell the mustiness of a vast auditorium.

When her small audience cheered and clapped her
afterward, she knew that she could never resign herself
to the life her mother had mapped out for her. She was
an Oldfield, and for her there was only the theater.

Chapter 3

The next morning the sunlight filtered through the tiny gap in the bed's rose brocade hangings, just as Janine had intended it to. Her room at Lavender Street always caught the full morning sun in the summer— She lay there, curled up warmly, imagining the freshness outside, and contemplating the crisp rashers of smoked bacon which she knew awaited her downstairs.

Someone drew the hangings back suddenly, and she smiled up at Peg. "Good morning, Mama."

"Good morning, sweetheart—see what a fine sunny day you've brought from Bath with you?"

"Ugh—don't mention Bath, I had just managed to put it from my mind."

"I do not believe Miss Tarrant's establishment is so very bad, Jan." Peg sat carefully on the edge of the bed, arranging her white silk wrap, but Janine noticed the slight trembling in the thin hands. Peg seemed weary already—

"Mama, I do not like Miss Tarrant *or* her academy *or* her young ladies."

"Nonetheless—"

"Must I remain there?" Janine reached out to put

her hand over her mother's. "I would rather be here with you all the time."

"You are my only daughter, and I intend that you shall have all the opportunities a young lady of breeding has."

"But I'm *not* a young lady of breeding, am I?" said Janine as patiently and gently as she could, for this matter meant so much to her that even in her mother's present state of health it somehow had to be said. "Mama, I want to be like you—can't we set the clock back to that time a year or so ago when you were happy for me to follow you?"

"Jan, you must bear with me—I will explain myself in good time. In good time. You should not be an actress, sweeting, because you *are* a young lady."

"Attending the academy makes me a lady?"

"No, that's not what I meant. Not what I meant at all," said Peg a little enigmatically, getting to her feet again to go to the window. The sun shone on her black hair, bringing out blue lights to echo the incredible blue of her eyes. Her skin was so pale it could have been fashioned from alabaster, and there was something fragile and ethereal about her as she stood there; something a world away from the lively, extrovert actress who enchanted London each night. "I *will* explain, Jan, darling, but not just at the moment. Tonight, after my show. I will make certain I accept no invitations, and then we can be alone and I will tell you everything."

"Everything?"

Peg smiled. "Yes, there is quite a lot to tell, perhaps. I want you to understand, sweetheart, to understand and accept. Now then, I must dress and go to the theater, there are certain parts of the performance which need a great deal of work to bring them up to scratch—"

"Mama, you should rest more, not rush out early to rehearse all day."

"I have a position to cling to, a crown to earn, if you like."

"No one can reach for that crown, Mama. Please, for me, rest a little more and give your health a chance."

"Dobby brought you scuttling from Bath, didn't she?"

"You should have told me yourself."

Peg went to the bed, dropping a kiss on the girl's forehead. "I'm perfectly well, just a little tired—I'm no eighteen-year-old maid now, am I? Now then, if David should call when I am out, you will be kind to him, won't you?"

"Yes."

"Oh, that one small word can be made to sound grudging at times."

"It is grudging, Mama. I don't like him and he doesn't particularly like me. But for you, I will try—but you must promise me something."

"What?"

"That you will take things a little more easy. Please, Mama."

Peg straightened. "I cannot, sweetheart."

"But—"

"No!" Peg spoke sharply, and then closed her eyes for a moment, putting her hand to Janine's cheek. "Forgive me, I didn't mean to raise my voice. We'll talk tonight, sweetheart, mm?"

Janine nodded, watching the elegant figure move toward the door. Alone again, she lay there thoughtfully. Something was wrong, and it went beyond Peg's poor health. But what was it? Perhaps tonight she would find out, but before then, she must attempt to persuade David Wolfe to use his influence on Peg. Someone must make her see that she must rest more.

Janine patted her lips with the napkin and folded it, sitting back. Crisp, delicious bacon always tasted better in this house than anywhere else. She looked around the small dining room with its green silk walls and striped brocade curtains. It was an intimate room, a room where the Chinese flowers and birds on the walls could almost be alive in this fresh morning light. Bowls of red roses stood on the table, before the fireplace and on the windowsills, and their perfume was everywhere. Outside the sparrows and starlings sang in the shrubbery and Peg's white peacocks strutted on the newly cut lawns. The roofs, spires and towers of London were beyond the high brick walls surrounding the gardens, making number seventeen Lavender Street seem a world of its own. Only the distant hum of the great city was there to remind her that she was in the heart of England's capital.

The butler came in, bowing slightly. "Lord Wolfe is here, Miss Janine."

"Oh. Thank you, Carter, will you show him in please?"

Carter bowed again.

Janine took a long breath and poured herself some thick black coffee from the delicate silver pot. Her moment of private pleasure was about to be ruined—

David was flicking the starched frills at his wrist as he came in, bowing elegantly before taking her hand and raising it to his lips. "You look more lovely than ever this morning, Janine. Blue is most certainly your color."

She removed her hand. "Thank you. Shall you take some coffee with me, my lord?"

"How vastly civilized that would be," he murmured as he sat down, lounging lazily in the nearby chair, watching her.

There was something unnerving about his eyes, the

way they seemed to wander all over her and yet always be able to meet her own if she looked up.

She handed him a dainty Sèvres cup. "I'm afraid my mother is already out, my lord."

"My name is David."

"I know."

He met her steady gaze for a moment, a faint smile on his fine lips. "Very well, as you wish. So, Peg has gone to the theater already."

"Yes."

"A dedicated *artiste,* worthy of the *monde*'s adulation."

"She works too hard."

"It would seem to me to be singularly pointless in trying to tell her that."

"You've tried?"

He stirred his coffee slowly. "But of course."

Somehow she didn't believe him. She found it hard to believe anything he said, and indeed had he said it was a fine, sunny day she would disbelieve the evidence of her own eyes after that— "Would you—would you try to persuade her to rest more, my lord?"

"I have."

"Please."

His sensuous eyes were warm. "Oh, how can I refuse such a plea?" he said softly, "or withstand such imploring eyes?"

"I am asking you simply and solely for my mother's sake, my lord."

"You think I have that much influence with the Divine Peg?"

"Yes."

"You flatter me."

"I doubt it." Janine stood, made uneasy now by the constant gaze. He had not looked away from her for one moment since sitting down— "My mother is very fond of you, my lord, and I am worried about her health. Surely you can see how unwell she is?"

He nodded. "I can see. We must devise a subtle plan, must we not?"

"Plan?"

"But of course. Between us we can make Peg rest more, I'm sure." He put down his cup and leaned back, his eyes half closed as he looked at her. "Dine with me tonight and we shall discuss how best we may do it."

She stared at him. An assignation with *him?* She would as soon meet a snake! "I have a prior engagement," she said at last, trying not to show the loathing she felt.

"Tomorrow then." He caught her hand suddenly. "Come now, Janine, I'm sure we could do well together, you and I." His thumb was caressing her palm.

He had no intention of persuading Peg to do anything, he was merely intent upon seducing her daughter! With a great effort Janine left her hand in his. Right, she would make an assignation, and let him wait there until kingdom come! "Very well. Tomorrow."

"Have you dined at the Orangery?" he murmured, more sure of her suddenly.

"No."

"Then you shall. I shall await you there at—say—eight?"

"I look forward to that." She removed her hand then, glad of interruption as the butler came in with a rack of toast. "Oh, no thank you, Carter, I've breakfasted sufficiently well. Well, I bid you good day, my lord."

David stood, glancing at her, but there was nothing in her face for him to gauge her by. He bowed and took his leave, and she picked up her napkin and wiped her hand on it, anxious to rid herself even of the memory of his touch.

"Dr. Venables?"

"Miss Oldfield, do sit down." The doctor ushered Janine to a green sofa in his drawing room. "A glass of wine?"

"Yes, please, for I think I shall need it."

He nodded, his smile fading. "Then I can guess the reason for your visit."

"You've attended Mama for so long now—"

"Since first she came to London. I even attended your birth, young lady. Yes, I can say I've attended your mother for quite some time."

"What's wrong with her, Dr. Venables?"

He sat down beside her, crossing his legs slowly and dusting an imaginary speck of dust from his old-fashioned breeches. "I don't know. She wastes away and is more weak and tired each time I see her, and yet nothing I prescribe for her seems to have any beneficial effect at all." He put his hand over Janine's suddenly. "My dear, I think you must be prepared for the worst, for I can see no hope ahead for her."

Janine closed her eyes to force the tears away.

He squeezed her fingers gently. "If she would rest more maybe the inevitable could be put off for a while, but in the end— And for whatever reason, she doesn't *want* to rest, even though I've counseled her as her physician. I've pleaded as a friend, demanded as her doctor, but to no avail. Something is driving her to further effort all the time."

"But what?"

"I was hoping that maybe you would know."

"No."

"Well, the one thing which seems to bring a glow to her is her—er, friendship, with Lord Wolfe."

"I despise him."

"There are many who do, my dear. A more hypocritical rake I've yet to meet."

"Rake, yes—but why hypocritical?"

The doctor's anger made him less than wary. "A true rake would not concern himself that his friends remained unaware his gambling debts were being paid for him by—" He stopped abruptly, flushing slightly.

"By my mother?"

"I did not say that," he said quickly, refilling her glass.

"But you nearly did." Janine stared across the room at the untidy desk with its clutter of documents and learned books.

"You are not to breathe a word to your mother, Janine, for I have said nothing and you are assuming—"

"And assuming correctly."

The doctor nodded at last. "Wolfe enjoys the glory of being known as the only man to enjoy Peg Oldfield's favor. The only man. Oh, what ill-placed love on your dear mother's part. Aye, he enjoys the glory and envy of other gentlemen, but has a horror of the truth coming out. In short, a hypocrite of the first order. A high-born louse."

"And Mama loves him."

"Yes. Unfortunately. However, his presence helps her, for it makes her try harder to remain as well as she can. He is a tonic for her, if you wish."

And he would betray that love with Peg's own daughter— Janine sipped the heady ruby-colored wine. "Dr. Venables, is there anything I can do to help her?"

"No."

She stared at him, her eyes large. "Nothing?" she whispered, "But—"

"Janine m'dear, it's only a matter of time. How long I cannot say, weeks, months—or maybe only days. I just don't know. I only wish I did."

She finished the wine and got weakly to her feet. When Dobby had told her, she had been able to withstand the truth somehow, but now, hearing Dr. Venables say it too— She was trembling all over, and he stood too, putting his arm around her shoulders. "Try to be strong, Janine, for she will need your strength."

She nodded, blinded by the tears.

As she reached the door he spoke again. "Only you and I—and Dobby—know the truth, Janine. No one else. And I must ask your discretion on the matter of Lord Wolfe, for I know only because your mother told me herself in a moment of weakness. If the tale got out, then she would know I had been less than discreet with her confidences, and I would never wish her to think that."

She smiled. "I won't say anything to her or to anyone else, Dr. Venables."

Chapter 4

Dobby came to stand next to Janine in the wings. The gay music echoed all around them as Peg swaggered on to the stage in her rakish clothes, and the audience stamped and cheered. The chandeliers high above the auditorium threw a pale, smoky light over the crowded seats, and gentlemen stood all along the aisles, each one trying to push closer to the brightly lit stage. The mustiness of the theater seemed to vibrate somehow, and Janine's skin tingled as she watched her mother. No one could bring a song to life or evoke an image as Peg Oldfield did. How magnificently blue her eyes were as she struck a pose before bowing as elegantly as any nobleman, her long leg shown to absolute perfection. Whistles of approval greeted each movement, and Dobby smiled at Janine.

"A good night, eh, Miss Jan? Look at her, I've seldom seen her perform better."

"She's wonderful, isn't she?"

Dobby touched the girl's arm. "And it's in your blood too, eh? Well, maybe what's to be will be, who can say?"

"I thought she seemed upset when I arrived earlier."

"She was an' all. That darned Toad was here and they had words."

"Lord Wolfe?"

"There any other toads about then?" Dobby sniffed, refolding the sequined costume she had over her arm. "They had words anyway, and he stomped off and left her crying in her dressing room. She locked herself in and wouldn't even let me in. Then, just afore you arrived, she came out, all made up and ready, and as if nowt had happened. Just like she is now, in fact. I don't know, truly I don't. What any sensible woman can see in that—that—! I can't think of a word bad enough."

Janine glanced at the little dresser. Did Dobby know about the gambling debts too?

The evening's performance came to an end, and in spite of repeated calls from the appreciative audience, Peg refused to go on stage again. In her dressing room she sat wearily by the dressing table removing her makeup, and Janine sat on the old sofa watching her. Dobby took away the costume as it was discarded, and Peg glanced at her. "Have there been any—messages for me, Dobby?"

"From him? No, ma'am."

Peg returned her attention to the mirror, wiping her eyes with an oiled cloth. She said nothing more on the subject of Lord Wolfe, but Janine could feel her unhappiness across the small room.

Dickon knocked at the door. "There's crowds on 'em out back, ma'am," he called, "and the Earl of Blaisdon's sent special to invite you—"

"I am receiving no one tonight, Dickon. Tell them I am spending the night here and they may as well take themselves elsewhere."

Dobby glanced in surprise at Peg, for Peg had always been very careful to please her many admirers, and this was a snub which was uncalled for. But Peg went on with her makeup and Dickon went away to deliver the message which was audibly unwelcome, even in the dressing room in the heart of the theater.

Peg stepped into the flimsy muslin gown Dobby held for her. "I am in no mood to fight my way home through adoring crowds tonight," she said, smiling apologetically at the dresser. "I just want some peace and quiet."

"And why not?" said the dresser briskly, pulling a hairbrush through the heavy black hair as Peg sat down again. "There now, that's you togged up nice and tidy again."

"What would I do without you, Dobby?" Peg smiled.

"You'd find no end on 'em wantin' my place, I knows that well enough."

Peg kissed the wrinkled cheek affectionately. "Until tomorrow then, Dobby. Good night."

"God bless, ma'am."

In the other dressing room the rest of the company laughed and chattered as Peg and Janine walked past, and they could hear the orchestra going over a sequence which had caused problems. The backdrops were being roped up and the winches and chains squeaked and echoed through the old building. By the door Dickon sat on his chair.

"They've all gone, Miss Peg," he said. " 'Tis raining again and they didn't need too much persuadin'."

"Thank you, Dickon. Good night."

"Night, ma'am. Miss Jan."

Outside it was indeed raining, and an anonymous post-chaise was drawn up by the door. The post-boy jumped down and opened the door for her.

The upholstery was threadbare and the horsehair stuffing decidedly lumpy in places as the two women sat down. Peg shifted uncomfortably. "I decided my own carriage was too conspicuous tonight."

"You've quarreled with David, haven't you?"

"Yes. Performing at all tonight was an effort after that, but now I could not possibly smile and flirt with admirers."

"Your performance tonight was superlative, you know that, don't you?"

Peg smiled. "Yes. A climax perhaps."

Janine watched her mother's face by the light from the street lamps as the old chaise rocked and bumped through London toward Lavender Street. The moving light brought out shadows which the daylight hid, a hollowness in the cheeks, a darkness beneath the eyes, a porcelain fragility which seemed to have settled more firmly over Peg Oldfield even in the one day Janine had been back with her.

Peg smiled at her. "We must talk when we get home, for it is only right you should know now. Ah, here we are. Oh, how I look forward to a rest in my favorite chair with my favorite champagne to sip."

Carter poured two glasses and thrust the bottle back into its ice bucket, wrapping the napkin around its neck before leaving the drawing room.

Peg watched the condensation appearing on the crystal glass for a moment. "Chilled to perfection, just as I like it."

"Carter knows your taste well."

"Well, Jan, here's to the future." Peg raised her glass. "*Your* future, for I have none."

"Mama—"

"No, I must admit that I am not immortal. Tonight's performance was my finest maybe because it was a farewell performance." Peg swirled the champagne thoughtfully. "I bow to the inevitable, and will rest more as you all so lovingly beg me. But coming to this decision tonight has cost me a great deal, sweetheart. Two years ago I may have been arbitrary, suddenly sending you to Bath and denying you the future on the stage that you wished for yourself. It was not arbitrary, sweeting, but something I felt I had to do for your own sake. I am no longer a rich woman, I have—invested my fortune somewhat unwisely. The coffers are virtually empty, Jan."

Janine stared at her in amazement. All the fortune she had acquired over years of being London's darling? Gone? Gone on settling Lord Wolfe's immense gambling debts—

Peg drained her glass of champagne and took the dripping bottle from its ice bath. "I possess this house, my carriage, my jewels and my clothes. But what money I have I receive each month from the theater manager, Starleigh. Jan, when I am gone, you will not have the fortune I wanted to leave for you, and I sensed that this would be so when I decided to send you for an education at Miss Tarrant's academy. Now you are a lady, poised and accomplished, and able to hold your own in—in society. You are my daughter and on stage you would be successful because of that fact—and because I know you are as talented as I am. But it's a hard life, sweeting, full of uncertainty, the whims of your audience, the jealousies of your rivals and so on. Maybe you would slip into its coat smoothly and comfortably—or maybe you would be forced to fight and claw as I had to once. I succeeded, but for every one like me there are hundreds who are never heard of again. If my fortune was behind you, then I could have rested easily about you, knowing that you would have had a comfortable life materially. But now—"

"I don't understand still, Mama," said Janine softly. "How does sending me to Miss Tarrant's make any difference?"

"Because now you can take your rightful place. Oh,

over the years I've denied that it's your rightful place, but now it must be."

"What? What rightful place?"

"I've never mentioned your father, Jan, because he and I made a sad mistake when we married. Oh, yes, don't look so surprised, for you are legitimate. I'm—or I *was*—a proud woman, and when the awful mistake Henry and I had made became apparent, and the dreadful gap between our respective characters and values became impossible to bridge—then I determined to bring you up alone. You were only three months old when I had my first chance to go on the stage, and I took my maiden name as a gesture to the world that I was independent, that I would succeed *alone*. And you have always been known by my maiden name too, but you are not an Oldfield, Jan, you are a Winterton. Henry Winterton left me when I was still carrying you, he left me penniless and homeless. But not nameless. You are Janine Winterton, sweetheart, and your family is wealthy and aristocratic. Their family seat is at Calworth in Yorkshire, and although your father is dead, your grandfather still lives there."

"Sir Adam Winterton?" gasped Janine, for she had heard of the Yorkshire family with their thousands of acres and vast fortune.

"Yes." Peg smiled faintly. "The old bear still keeps an iron grip on the reins. Oh, I never met him; Henry did not ever take me to Calworth, and I doubt that his family ever even knew that he had married. Henry died not long afterwards in a shipwreck somewhere out in the Atlantic." Peg leaned her head back, remembering. "Oh, he was a handsome man, Jan. His hair was fair and his eyes dark and roguish, and he wore his clothes with a dash to catch any woman's eyes. He could charm with a glance, enchant with a word. A flame to burn any finger. But beneath it all he was dissolute and selfish, cruel at times and sly at others. Dear me"—she smiled wryly—"how like him David is. That type must have some fatal attraction for me, it seems, for I am clay in their hands."

"You want me to go to Sir Adam Winterton at Calworth?"

"Yes."

"I can't!" gasped Janine. "I'd be like a mole hill on a fine lawn!"

"No, you wouldn't, sweetheart, you'd blend in as well as any gentlewoman. You're only half Oldfield, the rest of you is pure Winterton. You must go there when I'm gone, promise me that you will!"

"I—"

"Jan, I must have your promise."

"Mama, I cannot just go there and tell them I'm Henry Winterton's daughter, for they will never believe me!"

"They will, for I have my marriage lines to prove it. Henry and I were married nineteen years ago on the twenty-eighth of October, 1787, at St. Bartholomew's Church right here in London. The certificate is over there in the escritoire. Henry Winterton of Calworth Hall, Yorkshire, married Margaret Oldfield of Guildford, Kent. Promise me, Jan, that you will go there and at least try. For my sake."

Janine went to kneel by her mother's chair, taking her thin hand and resting it against her cheek.

Peg's fingers tightened. "I accept that if you are miserable and if the life is abhorrent, that you will come back here to try for a future on the stage. I accept that, but first you must try the alternative. Jan?"

Janine's tears were wet on her cheeks as she nodded. "I promise you, Mama," she whispered.

Peg closed her eyes, stroking her daughter's hair gently. "You can't know how much easier you've made me feel, sweetheart. Let us drink a toast, mm? To tonight's little talk?"

Wiping away her tears, Janine poured two more glasses of the champagne, and Peg raised hers. "Tonight."

"Tonight."

"If only—"

"Yes?"

"If only I had not quarreled with David today, then today would have been perfect. Ever the fool the woman who falls for a handsome face and practiced air. It began with poor Eve and the serpent, did it not?" Peg smiled as she drank the champagne in one gulp.

The next morning Janine woke with tired, sore eyes and a headache. She had cried herself to sleep, and now, when she looked in the mirror, the ravages of those hours of weeping were all too plain. She did not draw the curtains of the bedroom, but went to the dish of water on the chest of drawers, bathing her eyes in the coolness for a moment and then dabbing them dry with a towel. A dab of herbal salve might help a little and make her look less dreadful—

"Miss Janine?" Peg's maid tapped at the door.

"Yes, Miranda? What is it?"

The maid came in, curtseying neatly. She was like a little mouse in her gray seersucker gown and white apron, her fair hair tucked into a mob-cap. "Miss Janine, it's your mother—"

"What?" Janine felt the alarm rise immediately.

"She doesn't want to get up, Miss Janine. She just wants to lie there in her bed. And she won't take any breakfast, not even the nicely coddled egg Mrs. Banks did special. I poured her some of her favorite coffee, just as she likes it, but when I went back she hadn't touched it. Miss Janine, she's never done this, not in all the years I've been here."

"No, Miranda. I know. Let her be, she's not feeling very well."

"Very well, Miss Janine."

Peg remained in her bed all day, and by the early evening had shown no signs of any intention of getting up. She hardly moved, but stared all the while at David Wolfe's miniature which stood beside her bed. The weakness which encroached each day seemed to have drained her completely now, so that any movement was too great an effort and was therefore not attempted in the first place. It was as if, thought Janine, yesterday's final performance and the quarrel with David had proved the final straws for Peg's ailing constitution.

It was while she was sitting alone in the drawing room, taking her early-evening tea, that Janine suddenly remembered the dinner appointment with David Wolfe. He was responsible for so much of Peg's unhappiness. Janine thoughtfully stirred her tea, and that was the only sound in the room.

The Orangery lived up to its name. It was a glass-domed building in a park, lit inside with countless lanterns strung among the vines and citrus trees which grew in profusion in the humid atmosphere. The smell of damp earth, leaves and flowers was everywhere, but it was almost overcome by the smell of tobacco and food which was trapped within the fragile building. The chattering of the diners and the rattle of their crockery and cutlery vied with the music of the string quartet as Janine gave her name to the head waiter.

He threaded his way through the tables and greenery toward a dark corner, and as she neared the shadows, she saw David Wolfe seated at a discreet table for two, almost hidden by an overhanging fern. He stood as he saw her, and his dark, handsome face broke into a smile. "A lady not only of great beauty, but capable of being prompt."

The waiter took her light wrap and gloves and then pulled out her chair. As David ordered some wine, she wondered if she had perhaps dressed too cleverly. Her yellow silk evening gown had a very low *décolletage*, and showed off her shoulders magnificently, but now that she was seated opposite David Wolfe with his wolf's eyes, she thought perhaps a canvas bag from which only her head showed might have been more prudent.

He glanced at her coiled hair which tumbled in ringlets from a knot at the side of her hair, and then at the topaz drops in her ears. "The girl of two years ago has become a lady," he said softly as he poured the wine the waiter brought and then waved him away with a white-gloved hand.

But as he picked up his glass and waited for her to do the same, she shook her head. "I am not here tonight to dine with you, my lord, nor indeed to spend any more time with you than I can possibly manage."

His smile faded. "Why then?" he asked abruptly.

"Because my mother has not long to live and you, sir, are going to see that her last days are happy ones."

"And why should I put myself out?"

"Because if you do not, my lord, I shall see to it that the *monde* and his wife know how low you are. There will not be a drawing room in the land where your name is not ridiculed, nor a club where you may show your face without being greeted with derision. The man who let an actress pay his gambling debts. Oh, yes, I know about it, my *lord*. Look at me and know that I mean what I say. You pay court to my mother from now on as gently and lovingly as you can, or so help me—"

"Your point is taken, my dear." His face was cold.

She stood. "If you have not come to Lavender Street to see her by this time tomorrow night, sirrah, then my tongue will clack with a vengeance."

"So sweet a countenance, so vicious a heart."

"Vicious? That perhaps is a word to be written across your heart when you die. To be a kept woman is not quite the thing, is it? But to be a kept man must surely be the depths of contemptibility!"

She picked up her wrap and left the table just as the startled waiter came to take their order.

Chapter 5

It was a glorious July day as the funeral cortège wound its slow way through the crowded streets toward the church. The crowds were silent as Peg Oldfield took her last bow. The glass-sided hearse was drawn by four black horses with black caparisons and black plumes, and their harness shone and jingled. A black crepe pall covered the coffin, and on it two wreaths, one of Peg's favorite red roses from Janine, and the other an elaborate affair of white lilies and mimosa from David Wolfe.

Janine sat in the barouche, her face hidden by the veil pulled down from her beaver hat. The long weepers from its sides moved gently in the slight breeze, and the heavy pelisse and gown on black velvet felt stifling in the warmth. Opposite her, David sat in silence. He had done all she could have wished of him, fussing around Peg constantly, courting her and flattering her so that her last days had been happy ones. But since the night in the Orangery, he had not addressed one word to Janine.

The service was almost unendurable, and Janine's aching heart threatened to break with each dragging moment. Peg had gone forever. Her mother, her beloved mother—

David caught her arm and she looked around startled. The service had ended and the pall-bearers were carrying the coffin slowly out to the churchyard. She felt weak now that that final moment had come, and was conscious of David's arm supporting her.

By the graveside she looked around numbly at the mourners, from Dobby's grief-stricken face, to Dr. Venables' sad countenance, and then to all those fellow artistes who had so loved Peg Oldfield. And beyond, outside the churchyard, the clutter of fashionable carriages belonging to those of her admirers who had come to pay their last respects.

She couldn't pick up a handful of the earth, and it was David who did it for her. She felt that she could hardly stand suddenly as the spades scraped into the mound and the earth spattered over the coffin, and David put his arm quickly around her waist, holding her tightly.

He steered her through the churchyard toward the lychgate where the barouche waited. She could hardly see through the insistent tears, and it seemed that long after the barouche had left the church she could still hear the sonorous, dismal tolling of the bell.

At last the barouche turned into Lavender Street and came to a standstill. As she picked up her reticule, her handkerchief clutched tightly in her hand, he spoke suddenly.

"I take it that your threat no longer holds water?"

"You are no longer any concern of mine, my lord. I did what I did for my mother's sake and for no other reason. Your secret is now safe."

He studied her pale face behind the veil and then suddenly leaned to raise it so that he could see her properly, and she drew back immediately. He smiled faintly. "You are quite a woman, Janine Oldfield, in looks, in character and in strength. The Lord help London when you take to the stage."

She put a hand to open the door, but he put his own hand over hers. "I tell you this, Janine. Had I my time over again I would not have behaved as I did."

She snatched her hand from his touch. "You mean you would have behaved *honorably* toward my mother?" She felt like laughing out loud.

"No, I mean that I would not have courted your mother at all."

She stared at him as she realized his meaning. "Stay away from me," she breathed. "To the fashionable world you may be quite the fellow, but to me you are and always will be contemptible. Don't ever come near me or contact me again." She opened the door and got out before the waiting footman could do it for her.

She went inside and Carter closed the door behind her. David, Lord Wolfe, sat for a long time in the barouche without moving, and then he tapped the floor with his ivory-handled cane and the carriage moved away.

Carter came in with the tea tray and set it beside Janine in the drawing room.

"Carter, you have seen to the sale of my mother's jewels?"

"Yes, Miss Janine."

"Is there enough?" She put down her inky pen and looked anxiously at him.

"Enough to keep this house? Just about, Miss Janine. You say you will not be here?"

"No. I—I am going to Yorkshire for a while, I don't know for how long. Depending upon the outcome of my visit, I shall know my financial situation and whether I shall be able to keep the house going indefinitely. For the moment, however, some of the staff will have to go. Oh, I don't like dismissing anyone, Carter, but I cannot manage unless I do so. They will all have excellent references, of course. You might remain, and Mrs. Banks, and Miranda. And one of the kitchen maids, whichever one you think best. The rest must go."

"But what of the gardens, Miss Janine? They were your mother's pride and joy."

She glanced out at the rambling dark red roses around the drawing-room window. "I know," she said quietly, "but they must be left. There is no money, none at all. One way or another I shall keep this house, for it is my home, mine and Mama's."

"Yes, Miss Janine," said the butler, nodding. "I'll do what must be done."

"I shall go to Yorkshire in two days' time. I will be at Calworth Hall if you should need to contact me for any reason."

"Yes, Miss Janine."

He went to the door and she spoke again. "And, Carter, if Lord Wolfe should ever come here, he is not to be allowed in, is that clear? He is not to set one foot over the threshold of Peg Oldfield's house ever again."

"Very well, Miss Janine, you may rely upon me to see to your wishes."

When he had gone, she went to the escritoire and with her mother's key opened the little metal box which was kept there. Inside was a rolled document tied with a red ribbon. The marriage certificate of Henry Winterton and Margaret Oldfield. She read the faded writing. Winterton. Calworth Hall. The names were strange, unfriendly even.

The thought of going to Yorkshire, among strangers who would probably deny her, was daunting. Here in London, where Peg Oldfield's name was so beloved, there had already been offers from various theaters, each one anxious to secure the services of her daughter.

"But I gave my solemn word," whispered Janine to the silent room. "I promised Mama, and so I shall go to Calworth Hall. I *shall* try for her."

Chapter 6

Curlews called over the wild moorlands as the post-chaise traversed the widening track which led up from the dale. The skies were incredibly clear and blue, and the golden gorse blazed everywhere, standing out brightly from the subtle purple of the heather. As Janine looked out over the unknown landscape, she thought that it had been at least an hour since last she had seen a cottage, and there seemed to be no other travelers on this deserted road which led seemingly into nowhere.

On the brow of the moorland hill the coachman halted his weary team for a moment, leaning to speak through the grille to his passenger. " 'Ave to rest a while, miss," he said in his broad Yorkshire accent. "Tek a stretch on your legs awhile if'n you like."

She nodded, pushing open the stiff door and climbing down. The sweet, perfumed air seemed to dance on the hazy horizon, a soft blending of colors which made distance indeterminate. Without the noise of the chaise, the curlews' strange cries were louder, echoing over the lonely moors which stretched in all directions now that the dale could no longer be seen.

"How far is it to Calworth Hall?" she asked the coachman.

"A while yet. Not over yon rise, but over next, I reckon. Be there in an hour. Mebbe two. Can't say." He ran his fingers through his thinning hair, looking curiously at her.

"What's it like there?" she asked with a smile.

"Grand. Grander'n any other place I know of. Servants by the score, a stable full of blood horseflesh." He grinned. "Aye, and a cellar to make an emperor jealous, from all counts."

"And Sir Adam Winterton still runs it all himself?"

"The old feller? No, glad to pass it to his nephew. Leastways, not his nephew exactly, his stepnephew, if there be such a thing. Sir Adam's sister, Lady Serena—well, she married a feller as had a son already. Richard—Richard Stuart, that's who has the running of Calworth Hall nowadays. A damned Scot running good Yorkshire acres." He spat roundly over the edge of the chaise. "What that Lady Serena ever 'ad to go marryin' north of England's borders for, I don't know. Well, reckon team's 'ad a breather now and we can get on our way."

She climbed stiffly in again, praying that this would indeed be the last stage of her long, tiring journey from London. Six days of bumping and swaying over atrocious roads, each mile sending her spirits further into the depths. She looked at the never-ending moorland, so beautiful and timeless. So alien. The dark, exciting, claustrophobic world of a theater was what she yearned for, not this wild, magnificent freedom.

Her hands twisted nervously in her lap, clasping and unclasping. If she was not careful she would mark her white gloves on the window, for already she had almost reached up to wipe the grimy glass and had remembered in time. She must present the most excellent appearance possible when she first set foot in Calworth Hall. Had she chosen her toggery well? The neat blue spencer was finely stitched, and her blue-and-white-striped silk gown looked well, the blues being so close as to almost match. *Almost* match. Surely someone from Calworth would be *perfectly* matched. Still, it was the best she could do. She stretched out a foot to inspect her white stockings. Not a wrinkle, not a mark. And her little slippers were in pristine condition too. She glanced out the dirty rear window of the old chaise to where her luggage was strapped precariously to the boot. What she wore at present looked well enough, but that could not perhaps be said of most of her clothing. Mama had intended her to have a complete new wardrobe on leaving Miss Tarrant's academy, but now instead she must make do with what she already had. And one or two of her mother's gowns for special occasions—if indeed she survived at Calworth long enough to attend a special occasion. Somehow, in her heart of hearts, she had the feeling that her sojourn at the Yorkshire house would be short.

She sat back, closing her eyes and hoping that she could doze a little to pass the time which was dragging so awfully now. The ruse must have succeeded, for the next thing she knew was the halting of the chaise and the coachman's loud voice telling her that if she wanted her first look at Calworth then she had better look now.

The house straddled the small hill across the gorse-lined valley. A large, copper-decked dome rose from the center, and on either side stretched two immense wings, crowned by cupolas and rows of statues. There seemed to be countless windows to catch the afternoon sunlight, and each window, it felt to Janine as she climbed down from the chaise, seemed to be staring straight across at her. How bleak, desolate and forbidding it looked, how large and empty. The parkland stretching down to where the moor encroached was bare but for a few trees, and a small herd of red deer wandered in the long grass.

The coachman pointed with his whip. "That's the back you see; from t'other side it's right grand, with gardens, temples, ornamental trees and such like. I've been told there's sixty gardeners to see to it, so that'll tell you."

Sixty gardeners? She looked again at the gray stone building.

The coachman lowered his whip again. "We go along bottom of the valley—you can't see the road from 'ere—and then round over there. Just beyond there the woods begin. Aye, woods. Sir Adam's grandfather, or great-grandfather or sommat had more'n eight thousand saplings planted, and now they're a grand sight from the west. There's a red and purple pagedy—"

"Pagedy?"

"One of them Chinese things wi' dragons all over it."

"Oh, a pagoda."

"That's right, a pagedy. Sticks up like a sore thumb, so it does. There's bells and such like on it and when the wind blows they all set to noise. Right pretty it is. I've brought many a guest up 'ere in my time; I were coachman—*under*-coachman—afore my brother left me the business. Ah, I know a fair bit about Calworth Hall."

"It's so big."

"Aye, it's that all right. Still, you'll find plenty o' company there, there's that many staff you could raise an army, I reckon." He nodded at the house. "That Richard Stuart'll do all right, eh? And all on account of his dad's second marriage to Winterton. Trust a Scot to 'ave jammy fingers."

Janine stared at the house again for a moment. What would Richard Stuart be like? And Lady Serena who was her aunt? And Sir Adam?

"Hey, lass, what's your name, then?" asked the coachman suddenly.

She smiled suddenly as she looked up at him. "Winterton. I am Miss Winterton, Sir Adam's granddaughter."

His jaw dropped, and the clay pipe he had been about to light dropped with it, smashing on the stony track. "You *what?*"

"I am Sir Adam's granddaughter."

"Well, I'll be— That'll set cat among pigeons! 'Ere, you're 'aving me on, ent you! Sir Adam don't *have* no grandchildren!"

"Oh, yes, he does. Me. Well, shall we get on, then?"

He nodded, still staring at her.

The chaise jerked on its way, beginning the slow descent to the little valley. The deer bounded away as the carriage passed near them, and suddenly she could no longer see the house, for the slope of the land hid it from her. The track passed through a small ford where a beck babbled and chattered between ferns, and then suddenly there was little sunshine as the chaise entered Calworth Woods. Shafts of brilliant sunbeams danced in the glades where carefully chosen ornamental trees draped their foliage, some of it copper-colored, some crimson and some green. Strange white blossoms with sickly sweet perfume, rambling azaleas in purple, mauve and scarlet, and delicate silver birch grew together in planned confusion. It was like a dreamland to Janine as she stared out, somewhere seen in sleep but forgotten at daybreak.

The pagoda stretched from the treetops to her right. As the driver had said, it was red and purple, soaring skyward, its golden dragons flashing in the sun, but the sound of the chaise drowned any bells which may have been caught by the wind.

Through the trees she glimpsed two more exotic buildings, looking like marble temples. And then the woods seemed to end, although from the other window she could see that they continued to spread across the lower edge of the valley, but the track had broken out into the sunshine again—the sunshine and the fantastic formal gardens of the great house. In a book at Miss Tarrant's she had seen the wonderful gardens of Versailles, and now it was like seeing them again. Colorful flower beds, symmetrically arranged around lily pools where statues held fountains which splashed endlessly over the waters.

Now the house dominated everything again, stretching across its hilltop as if God had intended the hill for just that one building. She watched it as the chaise carried her ever closer, and inside she felt frightened suddenly. The mere size of the place was intimidating—

The chaise rattled around the wide circular drive before the wide stone steps which led to the great doors, so very far away it seemed. The wheels crunched on the newly raked gravel, and as it stopped she heard the tinkling waters of yet another waterfall in the center of the drive, a pool where fat cherubs flew on stone wings, and where the water pattered onto water-lily pads.

Slowly she climbed down, searching in her reticule for the coins with which to pay the waiting coachman.

As he took them he leaned closer. " 'Ere, you really a Winterton?"

"Yes."

"By, then you're goin' to set cat among pigeons," he said again, pocketing the money and flicking the whip over the reluctant team so that they strained to set the chaise in motion again.

"My baggage!" she called suddenly, and with a

barely concealed oath, he reined them in again, just as the great doors opened high above and, from the darkness behind, a man in blue and gold livery stepped out into the sunlight. He stood there for a moment, and both Janine and the coachman stared up at him.

Fastening his white gloves slowly, he began to descend the steps, of which there must have been at least fifty, so that Janine found herself listening to his buckled shoes on each one, her heart thundering. As he neared them she saw the neat white periwig with its black ribbon and the silken breeches of a footman. But his expression was haughty enough to be worthy of Sir Adam himself—

"You have business here?" he asked in a superior manner, still toying with his spotless gloves as he looked down his bony nose at Janine.

"Business?" she said, recovering as she bridled at his attitude. "No, I have no *business,* I have come to see Sir Adam Winterton."

"Sir Adam does not receive strangers."

"He will receive me." Anger was lending her authority, and the good lessons learned from Miss Tarrant were beginning to pay dividends. Her tone made the footman hesitate, glancing at her clothes and then at the poor post-chaise.

"And who am I to say it is?" he asked after a moment.

"I do not give my name while still standing at the foot of these steps," she said, sweeping past him, her bonnet ribbons flying. "Kindly have my baggage unloaded."

Oh, how very many steps there were, and how long she seemed to be in the view of everyone—if there had been anyone but the footman and the coachman—but at last the doorway was looming nearer.

At the top of the steps she stopped again, taking a

deep breath to calm her fluttering nerves. You're a Winterton now, she told herself, and with a final deep breath, she walked into the great entrance hall of Calworth.

Chapter 7

But once inside her nerve almost failed her, for nothing she had ever seen before could match the size and magnificence of that hall. There were six footmen, two on each side of the three double doors which led off the vestibule, and they too wore blue and gold livery. They were motionless, staring ahead like statues, and not one of them even glanced at the girl in blue and white who stood so uncertainly in the center of the great echoing space.

The floor was checkered with black and white marble tiles, and when she looked up she saw that the copper dome which was so visible from across the valley actually formed the roof of the hall. It was some fifty feet above her, plastered on the inside in gold and white, with a coat of arms in the center. Lunettes of stained glass allowed the sunshine in so that it lay with jeweled colors over the whole construction. The walls all around her were pale gold and white, and at the far end where two grand staircases flanked the hall, there were huge gold marble pillars stretching up to the floor above. Ahead of her, a Grecian archway opened on to a magnificent ballroom, and delicate chandeliers were

suspended around the edge of the vast space, their
crystal drops tinkling slightly in the draft of warm air
from the open doors. She shivered, for the marble
made everything so cool— Someone somewhere was
playing a harpsichord, a sweet sound drifting through
the endless rooms of Calworth Hall.

She felt numb with fear suddenly. Her hands were
cold and her mouth dry, but she forced herself to keep
an expressionless face; if the footmen could do it, then
so could she— How would Peg have coped with this
situation? *Coped?* Peg would have strode over the situation, rising above it in a manner as regal as any
princess! She had snubbed the Prince Regent himself!
Janine took a deep breath. "I'm Peg Oldfield's daughter," she told herself, searching her memory for all the
excellent lessons she had learned at Miss Tarrant's
academy.

Footsteps came steadily up some stone steps somewhere near, and she turned toward the sound, to see a
concealed door open and a man who was obviously the
butler came up from the kitchens. He paused as he saw
her, his shrewd eyes moving over her clothes and immediately classing her as someone who should *not* enter Calworth by the main doors.

"Yes?" he said coldly.

"Would you inform Sir Adam that his granddaughter is here?" she said in a voice Miss Tarrant would
have been proud of.

"I beg your pardon?" he said, caught off balance by
her words.

"I believe I spoke perfectly clearly," she replied. "I
wish to see my grandfather!"

"Er—yes." He came closer. "Sir Adam is not at
home at the moment, Miss—"

"Winterton."

"Miss Winterton. If you could call back at another
time—"

"Call back? Is it customary in this house to require members of the family to call again if Sir Adam is not at home? I will see my aunt, Lady Serena then."

He flushed a little, glancing at the silent footman who could hear every echoing word. "Lady Serena is not at home either, Miss—er, Winterton. Everyone is at Talbot Castle until later tonight."

"Then I shall wait. Will you have my baggage brought in? Where is the main drawing room?"

"The *state* room?" He stared at her, unable to decide what to do.

"If that is what it is called—yes. Well?"

"If you will follow me, Miss Winterton." He walked across the hall toward the nearest staircase, and she followed him up the black marble steps toward the landing above. Huge oil paintings hung everywhere, and she recognized several by Sir Joshua Reynolds, and one or two which she could have sworn were Rubens'. The butler walked past many elegant gold and white double doors, and paused at length by the last door, opening it and standing aside for her to enter.

The room was furnished in green and gold, with French furniture and paintings. Janine glanced at it and then turned to the butler. "I doubt very much that this is Calworth's state room."

The ruddy color on his thin face deepened. "Miss Winterton, I cannot show you to the state room until Sir Adam tells me that I may, for I have only your word that you are indeed his granddaughter."

She drew herself up. "Show me to the state room," she said coldly.

He closed the door and walked back along the corridor, throwing open two double doors which opened onto the long gallery of the house. Countless paintings, statues, elegant silverware and clocks lined its immense length, and above, the roof was formed of golden domes. Only one room opened from this gallery, and

the butler flung the doors open grandly to reveal the
state room beyond.

It was furnished in red and gold, silk cladding the
walls. The floor was covered by an Axminster carpet
which must surely have been designed and woven simply for this beautiful room. A great marble fireplace
stood opposite the door, and on the walls were at least
four large Van Dyke paintings. Chandeliers hung from
the painted ceiling, and golden candelabra were in each
corner of the saloon. The furniture was elegant, mostly
Chippendale, and the ornaments were Oriental.

The butler closed the doors behind her. "Shall you
take some tea while you wait?" he asked, obviously deciding that discretion was the better part of valor.

"Yes."

Alone in the room she sat on a crimson velvet sofa,
taking off her gloves and looking around again. Calworth. Could it possibly be that her father had lived
here? She sat there, a small, lost figure in the vast state
room. Since entering the house she had seen wealth on
a scale she had never seen before, not even in some of
the drawing rooms at Bath. The paintings alone must
be worth— She stopped. Only a parvenu would think
in that way. She must not look around with wonder in
her eyes, she must behave and look as if she accepted
everything as being perfectly normal.

When a neat maid in green seersucker and a white
apron brought her a tray of tea, she nodded and said
nothing more, ignoring the girl's obvious curiosity.

The teapot was silver, the porcelain Sèvres. Peg had
used Sèvres, but the quality and beauty of the dainty
yellow cup were breathtaking. She knew that that yellow color was rare and prized, and she hardly dared to
touch it. The sandwiches were cut so finely from such
white bread that she marveled at the skill and eye of
whoever had prepared them, and the cake melted in
her mouth so exquisitely that it almost seemed to dis-

solve. Everything about that lonely meal in the state room was intimidating, almost as if the eyes of the priceless paintings were watching with disapproval.

Afterward she passed the time by wandering around the room, looking at everything in detail, and feeling less and less confident as the hours dragged away into darkness. When the maid came in to light the chandeliers and candelabra, her courage was fast ebbing into the gloom outside. She stood by the window as the maids went silently about their tasks, but she could feel their constant, curious glances and knew that news of who she claimed to be had spread like wildfire through the staff of Calworth House.

Outside, footmen were carrying lights to ignite the oil lamps which were hung everywhere in the trees, and soon the formal gardens were gaily lit, and the playing of the fountains quite visible again. In Calworth Woods the pagoda too was ablaze with lights, the golden dragons catching the eye of any beholder.

Two horsemen rode toward the house, the one dressed soberly like a groom, the other a gentleman of high fashion. The horses stopped by the great steps and the light from the lamps fell across the two men. Janine watched the gentleman as he stood listening to the butler for a moment. He wore evening dress, a black velvet coat and beige breeches which emphasized his slender figure. The cut of that coat would make even Lord Wolfe envious, she thought. And if his hair was chestnut rather than the truly fashionable black, it still curled romantically around his face in the way which was the latest rage. He turned slightly, nodding, and his face was pale and handsome, although the effect was marred by the expression of anger she saw there.

He went up the steps then and passed from sight, leaving the other man to lead the two tired horses toward the stables.

Janine waited by the window. The gentleman, whoever he was, had obviously been sent for because of her. The vestiges of her failing courage seemed on the verge of vanishing completely as she looked around the crimson saloon again. But she was Peg Oldfield's daughter! She drew herself up. What would Peg have done? She would face anyone out, even Bonaparte himself!

The door opened and the gentleman came in. He paused by the door for a moment, looking coldly at her. Now that he was closer she saw that he was indeed handsome, and his long-lashed eyes were hazel, although dark with the anger she had seen earlier.

Abruptly he stood aside, indicating the door. "Get out," he snapped.

She raised her chin. "And why should I do that?"

"If you do not get out, I will have you thrown out!"

There was a Scottish accent there which told her he was probably Richard Stuart, her aunt's stepson. She stood defiantly by the window without moving. "I have no intention of going anywhere until I have seen my grandfather, Sir Adam."

"Sir Adam has no grandchildren, madam. So, if you please, you will get out of this house, off Calworth land entirely and with as much haste as you are capable of."

"No."

"Do not misunderstand me, the fact that you are a woman will not prevent me from forcibly removing you myself."

"And who might you be, sir?" she asked, employing her best Miss Tarrant voice.

"I am Richard Stuart."

"I am Janine Winterton."

He smiled faintly, managing to make it insulting and contemptuous at the same time. "Indeed. Your gall is almost impressive, madam. For the last time—"

"I am not getting out of anywhere at your command, Mr. Stuart. I am not here to see you, indeed you are not of the slightest concern to me. I therefore fail to see what business it can possibly be of yours what I do or where I am. Now, if *you* please—" She went resolutely to the sofa and sat down, her back straight and her chin high.

He closed the door suddenly and went to a table to pour himself a glass of cognac. "Madam, I was enjoying an evening with friends which was disturbed by news of your arrival. A winning hand, a royal flush no less, and I was forced to throw it in. I am not a patient man, nor is forbearance one of my virtues, and at this very moment I am feeling positively ill-humored. If you are who you claim to be—"

"I am not in the habit of lying, sir," she interjected.

"—then you can no doubt prove it," he went on as if she had not spoken.

His attitude rankled, and Peg's blood rose to the occasion. "I can prove it, and will do so. To my grandfather. You, sir, can go to the Devil for all I care."

He raised an eyebrow, swirling his glass. "You are no wilting blossom, are you? Indeed, you seem a modern miss with a great deal more clever enterprise than is surely seemly in a young lady. Very well, you shall see Sir Adam—when he chooses to return. In the meantime, by all means remain in state in the state room. Good night."

Surprised, she looked at him. "Good night."

His footsteps echoed along the gallery, a door closed and all was silent again. She sat back, her eyes closed for a moment. Outside, the darkness was inky and as she opened her eyes a flash of lightning lit the northern skies in the distance. Later there was a rumble of thunder. She closed her eyes again. How long would it be before her grandfather returned from Talbot Castle—

The crash of thunder startled her and she sat up, glancing at the clock on the mantlepiece. Two o'clock in the morning! She must have fallen asleep! Rain lashed down the windows, the wind thrusting it against the glass, and two jagged flashes of lightning illuminated the moors for miles.

The knowledge that she was not alone came suddenly and she turned with a gasp. An old man with a sallow face sat on a chair looking at her. His bald head was covered by an iron-gray periwig, and his thin, stooping body was encased in an excellent wine-red coat and oyster breeches. His bony hands rested on the top of a mahogany cane and he looked steadily at her without blinking.

"So," he said suddenly, "you claim to be Henry's child."

"I am his child, Grandfather."

"I gave you no leave to address me so familiarly, missy. Now, if you please, the proof of your parentage—" He held out a hand.

She took out the marriage certificate and gave it to him.

He perused it for a moment, his lips pursed, and then he nodded. "It would seem to be genuine enough."

"That's because it is."

"Why have you suddenly decided to come here?"

"Because I gave my word to my mother."

"Ah. Margaret Oldfield. Where is she?"

"She's dead. You probably know of her. Peg Oldfield."

"The actress?" He seemed surprised and then amused. "So, neither parent can give credence to your claim, can they?"

"No. I gave my word to my mother because she wanted me to come here and when she was dying I made the promise she begged of me. I do not want to be here, I don't like the thought of the countryside. I want to follow my mother on to the London stage, and believe me I have had offers from theater managers which were enticing. But a promise is a promise and that is why I am here."

"What exactly *was* the promise?"

"That I would come here, try the life of a Winterton, try very hard—and then, if I didn't like it, then I could consider myself free to take to the stage if that is what I want."

"And is it?"

"Yes."

"And still you keep your promise?"

"Yes."

"I admire that, Janine, it shows character and spirit. And loyalty. And ambition too, I suppose. In short, it proves to me that you are a very singular young lady. Maybe indeed you are my grandchild."

"I *am* Henry Winterton's daughter."

His shrewd pale eyes searched her face for a moment. "You interest me, Janine. Remain here. It would please me if you did."

"Do you believe me?"

He smiled, struggling to his feet. "Some decisions must be made carefully, Janine, and this is just one such decision. Your arm, my dear. Let us leave this drafty room and go to the library where my sister—your aunt?—awaits the outcome of this interview with great anxiety. You've met Richard, haven't you?"

The storm raged against the windows of the long gallery, and thunder broke overhead with such force that the house vibrated. Janine looked nervously at the rain as it sluiced down the panes.

Sir Adam smiled. "It is but a storm, Janine. You would be better advised being nervous about *my* rage if I find you to be an imposter."

"Then I am not nervous at all."

"So much faith in that piece of paper?"

"No, so much faith in my mother's word, Sir Adam."

They walked on past the silent statues and staring portraits.

Chapter 8

The door Sir Adam stopped by was open. It led onto a gallery which flanked the library. There was the distinctive smell of books everywhere as he ushered Janine ahead of him.

She looked down into the room below. A plump woman with henna-rinsed hair sat in a high-backed chair. She was perhaps a few years younger than Sir Adam, and their faces were very alike, with the same sharp, clever eyes. Her face was made up as harshly as any actress', and her corseted figure was pushed into a revealing yellow silk gown. Her hair, ears and throat glittered with diamonds which flashed and winked in the candlelight which swayed as the draft of the storm sucked through the house. The sound of the thunder was muffled here in the heart of the house; the books seemed to deaden everything as Janine at last began to descend the steps.

Serena watched her, her face set and expressionless.

Sir Adam's cane tapped down the steps behind Janine, and he complained under his breath about them being too steep and he'd have to have something done about them if he was to continue using them. She listened with half an ear, for she was aware of Serena's enmity. It was there in the stiff, set pose, the withering glance and the grip of the plump hands on the arms of the chair.

"Ah, good evening again, Richard," said Sir Adam suddenly, and Janine turned to see Richard Stuart standing by the book shelves beneath the steps.

He inclined his head, glancing momentarily at Janine. "Sir Adam."

"Well, Serena," went on Sir Adam, "you'll have some feminine company again for a while."

The plump face twitched. "You *believe* this imposter, Adam?"

"I merely ask her to be my guest for a while, Serena. I see from your face that you are about to be in a miff, and the very thought appalls me at this time of night. Janine will remain under this roof, at least for a time. You, Serena, must accept it."

"And what of Richard?" asked Serena swiftly.

"Well? What of him? Mm? Have you a complaint, Richard?"

Richard closed the book he was glancing through, and replaced it on the shelf. "Complaint? And why would I complain about your choice of guest, Sir Adam?" His hazel eyes flickered disinterestedly at Janine.

"Why indeed." Sir Adam smiled, his eyes almost hooded as he glanced around at the three faces. "Well, that's my long day finished, and my bed calls me. Janine, I have instructed Witherspoon to have the Chinese room prepared for you. Ah, here he is now. The room is ready, Witherspoon?"

"Yes, Sir Adam."

"Go with him then, Janine, and good night to you."

"Good night—Grandfather."

He smiled again. "With so sweet and lovely a face and so winning a smile, I think I shall enjoy being persuaded by you, my dear. Oh, Witherspoon, did you find a suitable maid among the endless staff?"

"Yes, Sir Adam. Cally Arkwright. She—er—she attended Lady Angela." The butler's eyes flickered to Richard, whose face was still.

"Ah, yes, Cally. Damnable chatterbox like all the blasted Arkwrights, but a good little wench. Off with you then, Janine. I will see you at breakfast."

She nodded, going back up the steps to where the butler waited.

When she had gone Serena turned on Sir Adam. "How *could* you! That little slut has no—"

"Serena, I will not have Janine referred to as a slut. She certainly does not appear to me to be such a creature, and besides it is surely slanderous to say so. She is my guest—as you are yourself, if I may remind you—and I will not be amused to find that you have been behaving badly. Is that clear?"

His sister's eyes flashed angrily, but she nodded. "*Perfectly,* Adam. I merely trust that after all the work my son has put in here—"

"You may rely on me to do the proper thing by Richard, Serena."

Richard unbuttoned his gray waistcoat and sat down, crossing his long legs before him. "I expect nothing, Sir Adam. I am, as ever I was, merely your sister's stepson. A Stuart, not a Winterton."

Serena snorted. "And what real proof is there that that—that—*girl* is a Winterton?"

Sir Adam sighed. "She has a marriage certificate. Henry, it would seem, married Peg Oldfield."

"The actress?" gasped Serena in horror. "That gel's an *actress'* daughter?"

"Yes."

Serena closed her eyes faintly. "An *actress* at Calworth," she murmured.

Richard smiled. "That explains a great deal," he said, "a very great deal."

"I am not in the mood for enigmatic utterings, my boy," said Sir Adam, going to the steps. "Good night to you both."

"Good night, Sir Adam."

Serena said nothing, scowling at her brother's back as he went up the steps. When he had gone she looked at her stepson. "This could mean losing everything—"

"I am aware of that, Mother. An actress. Well, why not? And now, *I* shall retire too." He got up. "Peg Oldfield was a woman of strength and tenacity. One wonders if that strength and tenacity have been passed on to her daughter."

"One look at her will tell you they have."

He nodded. "Maybe."

Janine followed the butler through the house. Away from the almost claustrophobic closeness of the library, the sounds of the storm could be heard again, raging over the wild moors, bending the gorse and making deep puddles on the rutted track. She paused by a window, looking out. How far away London now? A million, million miles—

The butler cleared his throat, and she walked on again.

The Chinese room was warm and cozy, with a fire crackling in the hearth and throwing warm lights over the furniture and walls. Dragons writhed around the marble fireplace and on the legs of the tables and chairs. They were even around the gilt mirror, along the andirons and fender and around the gold-painted cornice. Had one raised its fierce head from the heart of the fire, Janine thought she would not really have been surprised. The walls of the room were the softest of apple greens, and on its silken surface was painted a Chinese garden with pagodas, lakes, trees, flowers and birds. The polished wooden floor was scattered with Oriental rugs whose colors trembled in the gentle firelight. It was a beautiful, exquisite room with its rosewood furniture, but the crown of the room was surely the bed itself. It was an elegantly proportioned fourposter with golden brocade hangings and counterpane, both woven with the almost inevitable dragons. But above it the canopy was carved and painted to look like a pagoda. Behind the bedhead, the tester was cloth-of-gold, stitched painstakingly with the Winterton coat-of-arms.

The butler bowed. "Good night, Miss Winterton."

"Good night, Witherspoon."

She waited until he had gone, and then went to the bed, running her fingers over the hangings with their golden tassels and fringes.

"Chippendale, Miss Janine," said a voice, and she looked around to see a maid standing there with a bowl of carnations in her hands. She was small and very fair, with her hair twisted in thick plaits on either side of her head. Her skin was freckled and her eyes pale blue, and at the moment round and large and somehow even more nervous than Janine herself felt.

"It's very beautiful."

"It were for Lady Angela—" The maid carried the carnations to the bedside table. Then she straightened her apron and bobbed a neat curtsey. "Cally, Miss. Cally Arkwright."

"I'm pleased to meet you, Cally."

"I attended Lady Angela."

"Presumably Lady Angela Talbot of Talbot Castle."

"Yes, Miss Janine."

"Don't look at me like that, Cally, you can't be more nervous than I am," said Janine suddenly, for the maid was almost quivering as she stood there, standing first on one leg and then the other.

"Begging your pardon, Miss Janine."

The wide-eyed agitation was still there, and the maid almost ran across the room as Janine began to unbutton her spencer. Janine stood there as the maid slowly undressed her. No lady at Calworth House obviously did anything for herself, and it crossed her mind as she watched the busy-fingered maid that perhaps even an itch would be scratched for you. Cally unfastened Janine's gown, but as she did so she dropped the spencer. Automatically and without thinking, Janine bent to retrieve it, but at the same time so did Cally, and with a crack their heads struck. They both straightened, wincing, a hand to the bruise. They looked at each other for a moment, and then both burst into laughter at the strange sight they must present, and the ice was broken. Cally relaxed, and so then could Janine.

"Oh, Miss Janine, I thought as you'd be another like Lady Angela—oooh that'd be awful. Beggin' your pardon for sayin' it."

"Was she that bad then?"

"A regular tartar she were, always finding fault no matter what. Get this, mend that, pick up t'other, haven't you brought so-and-so? Had me run off of my pins, she did."

Janine glanced at the bed. "But why was she to have had a room here?"

"She were to marry Master Richard, it were all arranged. Then she went to London to stay, got the smallpox and that were that. They reckon the pock marks would've been awful had she lived, and she were that proud of her looks that maybe it were just as well."

Janine found herself wondering if Richard Stuart had loved his Lady Angela, or if she had loved him. He was very handsome and assured, the sort of man any woman would wish to be seen with— The thought surprised her, and she sat down at the dressing table, staring at her reflection. Richard Stuart was very attractive—an arrogant, overbearing Scotsman. And very attractive in spite of that—or maybe because of it.

"Is it true, Miss Janine?"

"Mm?"

"That you're Peg Oldfield's daughter?"

"Yes."

"Well, I never." Cally stopped brushing her hair. "My brother Jethro saw her once, he's the only Arkwright bar me as 'as ever been to London. I went with Lady Angela once or twice. Didn't like it after Yorkshire, all poky and dirty it were. But Jethro said Peg Oldfield were the grandest thing he'd ever seen, she danced and sang like a angel, he said."

An angel? Peg had hardly looked like *that*— "I'm glad he liked her."

"Thought she was beautiful. He bought a little bunch of violets and sent it to the theater with a little note. He can't write well, can Jethro, but he did his best on account of he were that impressed and wanted to tell her so. He said there were huge baskets of grand flowers, great bouquets and such like all arriving at the back door, and he almost took his violets away again. But he plucked up his courage and handed them to the man at the door. She sent word out, telling him she were charmed with the violets and thanking him. Just him, out of all them fancy nobs. Didn't know where to put himself, did Jethro. Worshiped her after that he did. He broke down and cried like a babby when he 'eard as she'd died not long back— Oh, beggin' your pardon, Miss Janine, I didn't mean to remind you—"

"That's all right, Cally. My mother would be more proud of having an honest admirer like your brother than of having a hundred wealthy gentlemen clamoring for her merely because Peg Oldfield was the rage. She was like that."

"From what I've heard Jethro say, you must look a

lot like her. You're just as beautiful, you must be."
Cally trailed her fingers through the thick glossy hair.

Janine blushed. "It's kind of you to say so, but I
don't think I can hold a candle to my mother."

Cally put down the brush. "Shall you be wanting
some supper?"

"No, I'm not hungry. But a glass of hot milk would
go down well."

"I'll fetch it right now."

When the maid had gone, Janine went to the window to look out at the storm. The room looked over
the back of the house toward the rough parkland
where she had seen the deer earlier in the day. The
deer were still there, huddled together beneath the
spreading branches of an ancient oak tree, and the
storm was still doing its worst as the night dragged on
toward dawn. Lightning cut the distant skies again as
she opened the window to breathe the damp, fresh air.
The rain was softer from this side of the house, for the
wind was on the other side. There was a smell of herbs
from the kitchen gardens—lavender, rosemary and
thyme, their rain-bruised leaves releasing the strong
perfumes into the night. She leaned out, enjoying the
feel of the raindrops on her face.

A movement caught her eye almost directly below
and she looked down to see Richard Stuart walking
slowly by himself. He had discarded his costly coat and
his white shirt stood out in the darkness. The white
linen clung to his body, and his hair was soaked, clinging around his face. He walked slowly, as if deep in
thought. What would make him walk out on such a
night, she wondered, and at such an hour? By an ivy-
clad wall he paused in the shelter, and after a moment
he lit a cigar, leaning back against the wall, staring at
the moors.

She watched him, remembering her earlier thoughts.
Yes, she was drawn to him. But he seemed to have

nothing but contempt for her, that much was apparent in what he said, his gestures when near her and probably in his thoughts if she could have crept into them. She was vulnerable suddenly, in a way which was totally unexpected. All the various problems and situations she had tried to prepare herself for, but not this one. The cigar glowed in the gloom and a drift of the wind carried the smoke to her window.

He looked up suddenly as if he sensed that she was there. For a moment their eyes met, and then he casually threw his cigar down and walked away. She closed the window. She would not let herself be vulnerable, nothing on earth would let her reveal the chink in her armor. Richard Stuart would think her as contemptuous of him as he was of her.

Chapter 9

The next morning she was careful to dress as suitably as possible. She put on a dainty pink muslin gown, and Cally dressed her hair up in a knot at the back of her head. There was no locket or bracelet to wear as she had sold them all in order to keep the house in Lavender Street. Did she look too bare?

"No, Miss Janine," answered Cally when asked, "you look just grand. You don't need no jewels, honestly you don't."

"You'll have to tell me where the breakfast room is."

"The footman will take you, Miss Janine. They always escort the ladies to their meals."

"Oh."

Sure enough, a short while later a blue-and-gold-liveried footman duly presented himself at her door. She followed him through the long corridors toward her first breakfast at Calworth.

The breakfast room was on the ground floor, and as she descended one staircase into the hall, she looked across and saw Richard Stuart descending the other one. He nodded coolly at her, barely a greeting at all, and she returned the salute with even less interest—outwardly. At the door of the breakfast room he stood aside for her to go first, and it was as if he were ushering a maid through.

Sir Adam and Lady Serena were already there. Serena was devouring a plate of deviled kidneys, and she paused only to look up at Janine and scowl. In the daylight her hennaed hair looked garish and common, although no doubt she would have been horrified to know that was what Janine thought. Her ample bosom was oozing out of her tight red gown, and even at this early hour she was glittering with diamonds. Sir Adam smiled as he stood to greet Janine, crossing the room to take her hand.

"Ah, Janine, how refreshing you look."

If it had been a jab at his sister, it went over Serena's head. He led Janine to the long sideboard where a line of silver-domed platters waited, containing a bewildering array of steaming dishes ranging from Serena's deviled kidneys, through various fish dishes, to huge beefsteaks. She did not feel particularly hungry, but knowing that Richard would have to wait until she had chosen, she deliberately took her time, pondering her choice for a long time before deciding against them all and asking merely for some toast and lime marmalade. If her behavior irritated him, he showed nothing, not by a flicker of an elegant eyebrow, but she took solace in the thought that she must have annoyed him just a little. As she sat down she felt she had scored a small point and pulled back his lead even if by only a little.

Sir Adam sat down when Janine was seated, picking up his napkin again. "Do you ride, my dear?"

"Ride?" The thought filled her with horror.

"Dear me, that won't do. Everyone at Calworth rides. All Wintertons especially."

"Then I shall have to learn," she said immediately.

He smiled. "Richard will attend to your tuition, won't you, Richard?"

Richard put down his beefsteak and flicked his coat-tails as he sat down. "Must I?"

"Have you a good reason for not being gallant?" asked Sir Adam, sitting back, looking at him.

"Not a good one, no. Very well, I will teach Miss—er—Winterton to ride."

His tone was a snub and she felt goaded. "It's perfectly all right, Mr.—er—Stuart. I would much prefer to be taught by someone who is at least interested in whether I succeed on horseback or not. A groom maybe."

A vague color stained his cheeks for the first time and his eyes darkened as he looked at her. "I said I would undertake to teach you, and that is what I will do."

Sir Adam glanced from one to the other. "Lady's a suitable mount for her, Richard."

Serena sniffed, finishing the endless kidneys at last. "Damned nag's half dead," she said. "No one could possibly *not* ride it! Not even—" She didn't finish the sentence.

Sir Adam stirred his thick black coffee. "You're not doing anything particularly time-consuming today, are you?" he asked Richard.

"Seeing the bailiffs about rents, and interviewing the fellow who wants the tenancy of Edge Farm. Apart from that—"

"I don't want that farm going to just anyone, it's prime land—"

"I am aware of that," said Richard. "I don't think I've placed your tenancies badly as yet."

"No, you're an excellent manager, my boy. Don't know where I'd be without you these days—" The sentence hung pregnantly in the air, and Janine was aware of an immediate atmosphere between Sir Adam and his sister. If Richard sensed it, he revealed nothing, but went on with his breakfast.

Serena got up suddenly, her chair scraping. "I'm driving over to see Virginia this morning," she said shortly, her face and body stiff.

"Sit down, woman. Even Virginia Abingdom don't want visiting at this hour. Stop your damned bristling, Serena, it's cursed irritating at the start of the day."

Serena flushed and sat down again.

Sir Adam looked at Richard. "Do your tasks this morning and take Janine out this afternoon."

"Very well."

Janine scraped butter on her fly's-wing toast. "If it's not convenient, Mr. Stuart—" she said, intent upon making him repeat his assurance.

"It's perfectly—er, convenient, Miss Winterton," he said without glancing at her.

Serena suddenly got up again, walking from the room without a word. Sir Adam finished his coffee in a gulp and got slowly to his feet, picking up his cane. "Damned fool of a woman," he muttered. "Until later then, Janine, Richard."

Alone in the room with Richard, the silence became almost overpowering. Each mouthful of the crunchy toast seemed to make a terrible noise, and in the end she stopped eating.

The moments passed and he glanced briefly at her. "Pray go on eating, Miss—er, Winterton—I assure you I cannot hear as much as you seem to think."

She poured herself some coffee, wishing she could think of a suitable retort, but none was forthcoming. She sipped the coffee, glancing at him from beneath lowered lashes. This morning he wore a pale gray coat. Its cut was as excellent as the other one had been. It reeked of Bond Street, she decided. He was perfectly turned out, in the very tippy, as Peg would have said. His cravat was a wondrous creation which should have taken his valet hours, but which probably was merely a couple of skillful twists of his own wrist. She could not imagine him suffering a valet to fuss around him. His complexion was pale, with no rouge as Lord Wolfe used, and after the soaking it had received the night before, his hair was ruffled and almost untidy, but even that managed to look contrived. A spot on his nose would have helped to mar the dreadful perfection, but there was no spot.

"I *do* have all my teeth?" he said suddenly, sitting back. "Shall I now survey you instead?"

"I was merely wondering if all Scotsmen were as boorish as you are," she countered.

"Indubitably. But, I ask myself, are all women as pushy as you?"

"Pushy?" she gasped, taken aback at the choice of such a word. "I'm not pushy."

"No?" he murmured, folding his napkin.

He had only said it to irritate her and he had succeeded, and she realized it too late. Her barbs only struck home occasionally, but his seemed to wing inevitably to a bull's-eye each time.

He was still looking at her. "You've been at this table for at least half an hour, but you have not once looked at Henry Winterton's portrait."

"My father? Which portrait is of him?" She looked around the paneled walls at the various canvases.

He looked surprised. "Surely you know your own father?"

"Why should I? He left my mother before I was born and he did not return."

He pointed at the portrait over the fireplace. Henry Winterton's rakishly handsome figure was painted against a background of Calworth House. He was just as she had imagined him from Peg's description; his eyes had a wickedly roguish shine, and there was a deb-onair carelessness in the way he leaned against a broken pillar, his hat in his hand, the other hand restraining a large wolfhound.

"A rogue, philanderer and louse of the first order," said Richard, looking at her again.

"It would perhaps take one to recognize one."

He smiled as if faintly amused. "Why have you kept silent about being a Winterton for so long?"

"I did not know I was a Winterton, I assumed I was Peg Oldfield's illegitimate child, if you must know."

"But suddenly, after years of discreet, heroic silence, Sweet Peg comes forth with the truth?"

"Yes. She had excellent reasons."

"But of course," he said dryly.

She put down her cup and stood. "At what time do you wish me to present myself for my riding lesson?"

"What time do you wish?"

"I don't *wish* at all, Mr. Stuart."

Again the irritating smile. "Ah, but we must please Grandpapa, mustn't we?" He got politely to his feet. "Would three o'clock be suitable?"

"As suitable a time as any," she snapped. She had been determined to remain cool and aloof, but she had failed abysmally.

He spoke again as she reached the door. "I trust that you possess a riding habit, Miss Winterton—Peg Oldfield's antics are hardly the thing for Calworth."

Her face was flaming. "But gutter manners apparently are, Mr. Stuart." With a great effort she refrained from slamming the door behind her.

Cally was waiting in her room, and the maid watched in amazement as her new mistress came in, picked up a cushion and threw it furiously against the wall.

"Miss Janine?"

Janine breathed in slowly and heavily. "Damn Mr. Richard Stuart!" she said.

"Aye, a dry one is Master Richard."

"A prig! Well, that's my temper over and done with. I'd like a golden sovereign for every cushion I threw at Miss Tarrant's."

"Miss Tarrant's?"

"An academy for young ladies." Janine put on an affected tone and minced around the room for a moment. "In Bath, don't you know! 'Pon me soul, stap me and what? Eh?"

Cally burst into delighted laughter. "Oh, Miss Janine, that's just how some of them are! *Just* like it. Ee, there's a lot of Peg Oldfield in you, isn't there?"

"Too much at times," agreed Janine, "especially her stubborn streak. Cally, I am to be taught to ride by Mr. Hoity-Toity himself, and I have no riding habit. Is there one anywhere in this place, do you think?"

"A riding habit—" The maid thought for a moment. "Well, there might be one of Lady Catherine's—your grandmother. Sir Adam kept all her things when she died all them years ago, there's sure to be a riding habit there, she were never *off* a horse. Mind, it'll be old-fashioned—"

"So long as it's *decent*."

"Oh, it'll be that all right."

"In the attics? Well, let's go and take a look, mm?"

"*You* go up there too?"

"Yes, it will be something to do. Oh, no one will see, come on."

Cally led her out of the room and across the long gallery to a small door halfway along it. They went up the narrow, little-used steps to the musty rooms above.

Cally squealed suddenly and halted as a shadow moved in one of the rooms. The two women shrank back as scuffling, rummaging sounds came from the room, but then Janine sighed with relief as she heard a familiar noise—the tap, tap of Sir Adam's cane.

He turned sharply as she went into the room. He stood by an old chest, a gold-clasped, leather-bound book in his hand, and for a moment he looked angry. But then he smiled. "I did not hear you, my dear."

She glanced at the chest. It had initials painted on it and the Winterton coat-of-arms. H.W. Henry Winterton? He closed the chest and locked it again. "What brings you up here, Janine?"

"Mr. Stuart says I must have a riding habit."

"Indeed you must."

"Well, I haven't, and we thought—*I* thought— If there is a riding habit among my grandmother's things, may I please borrow it? I promise to take great care of it."

His pale eyes rested on her for so long that she thought he was going to ignore the question, but then he nodded once. "If Catherine's clothes are in any state, my dear, then of course you may borrow what you wish."

"Thank you, Grandfather."

"Not yet, my dear. Not quite yet."

"Don't you believe me?"

He put a thin hand to her cheek suddenly. "Sometimes I do, and by God I desperately want to. But I must be sure beyond a doubt. I'm an old man, and a beautiful granddaughter takes a little getting used to. Catherine's trunks are in the next room."

They listened to him going stiffly down the narrow steps.

Cally looked at Janine. "I thought he were going to be mad for a moment."

"So did I. Is that my father's trunk, Cally?"

"Master Henry? It must be, Miss Janine, there's no other Winterton with those initials."

Janine stared at it. What had her grandfather been looking for? Maybe the book?

Lady Catherine's riding habit was at least twenty years old, older than Janine herself. Cally held it up after shaking it. It was dark blue, formed to look like a tightly waisted jacket and full long skirt. It was trimmed with scarlet lapels and cuffs, and with it were a shirt and cravat, and a wide-brimmed hat with three enormous dark blue ostrich feathers. Janine looked at everything in dismay. "Oh, Cally, it's—it's *ancient!*"

"Reckon I've not seen nowt like afore!" agreed the maid.

"Look at that tiny waist! It'll cripple me to corset myself that much, she must have been *tiny!*"

"Not that tiny, looking at everything else bar the waists. No, look here, look at this corset thing. She must have been laced till she could hardly breathe."

"I can't wear any of it! I'll wear an ordinary dress."

"You can't, Miss Janine, you'll show all your legs and things. It's not proper. Side saddles are awful for that. We'll get you into all this, don't you fret."

"Aye," said Janine in a Yorkshire accent, "but will you get me out alive, that's what I want to know."

Chapter 10

"A bit more," said Cally, pulling the laces even tighter.

"I can't breathe!"

"Just a bit, and that's it!" Cally almost squeaked as she tugged, her teeth gritted.

Janine let go of the bedpost at last and slowly straightened. The corset held her rigidly and when she looked at her reflection in the looking glass she saw that she now had an hourglass figure. She walked a few steps. "It squeaks!"

"No it doesn't, you're imagining it. Now then, step into the habit."

"The shirt, we've forgotten the shirt."

Eventually she was ready. It was like looking at a figure from the past. With the hat throwing her face in shadow, it felt strange to look at the reflection and know that it wasn't a painting. Cally stepped back to look at her. "Well, I don't know," she said after a moment. "We go on about waists being out and all that, but I reckon that looks really grand. A tiny waist. Ee, I wish I had one."

"You wouldn't if you were laced into this contraption. It's bad enough just standing here, but I've got to get on some horrible nag and do strenuous things such as stay on!"

Cally giggled. "Every window in the house will have someone peeping out to watch you."

"That remark does *not* help!" Janine took off the hat suddenly. "My hair's in the way. Didn't they wear their hair loose with these hats? Isn't there a portrait out in the gallery of someone in one?"

"Yes, Miss Janine. That's Lady Alexandra. You're right, her hair is all loose. Here, let me unpin it."

With her hair free the hat felt more comfortable, but it was the only thing which did. The stable clock struck three and she took a deep breath to fortify herself. "Cally," she said, "have something suitably intoxicating waiting for my return, I have a dreadful suspicion I shall need it. For a variety of reasons."

Her grandfather was waiting in the hallway as she appeared at the top of the staircase. He turned as he heard her and his face changed, his lips parting. Her face was in shadow again because of the hat, and as she neared him he came to stand at the foot of the staircase, still staring up at her.

When she reached the bottom he smiled gently. "It—it was like going back," he said so softly that she could hardly hear him. "Like seeing Catherine again after all this time. The tilt of the head, the movement of the body. Just like her."

He took her hand and kissed it, and she looked into his face. "How long ago was it, Grandfather?"

"March the second, 1790. At eleven o'clock in the morning. A gray and dismal day. She'd been thrown from her horse a week earlier—oh, not in that costume, in another one which I burnt for its crime. A week she lingered, my sweet Catherine. I loved her very much. I'm an irascible old fellow now, but over the years I've not lacked for attention from the fair sex—but there's been no one I'd even glance at, no one to come even close to being as special as Catherine."

"Can you hear me creaking?" she asked, determined to lighten his sudden poignant sadness.

"Eh?"

"The stays," she whispered. "I'm sure they creak, but Cally swears they don't."

He laughed then, slapping his leg delightedly. "If they do, m'dear, it'd be music in me old ears after all this flowing looseness.we get these days."

She gathered the cumbersome, heavy skirts and went out the main doors to the top of the wide steps. She glanced around, half expecting to see crowds of eagerly waiting servants, all intent upon watching the charade, but there was no one there. She began the descent, conscious of the dragging of the skirts behind her. She wanted to inhale really deeply, but the corset willfully prevented her, taking an apparent pleasure in digging in if she was foolish enough to attempt anything untoward.

She duly presented herself in the stableyard, exactly ten minutes late. Richard was standing by a loose box with one of the grooms, leaning on the door, looking in at the mare and foal inside. Several of the grooms halted in amazement as Janine walked resolutely across the cobbled yard toward him, and one of the older men seemed especially taken aback. She heard him muttering as she passed.

"God above, I thought it were her ladyship come back!"

Richard's excellent, high-fashion turnout seemed all the more pronounced to Janine as she halted at last. She knew he'd heard her coming, and she knew too that he'd take his time turning to look at her. And so she waited, without saying a word.

At last he did indeed turn, and his face changed almost comically for a moment. "Good God!" he murmured.

"You, sir, are fashionable now, I was fashionable then. A riding habit you wanted, and a riding habit you've got."

He looked at her from head to toe. "What is your life expectancy in that, Miss Winterton? Half an hour? Three quarters?"

"It feels like a lot less. Where is my funereal nag?"

He nodded at the groom, who hurried away. She went closer and peeped into the loose box. The bay mare's ears flicked forward, and the nudging black foal looked up from feeding. Janine watched, enchanted. "What's he called?"

"He's a she. Guinevere."

"I didn't know *he* was a she," she protested. "They all look the same!"

He raised an eyebrow. "Do we indeed? Then I begin to wonder what lamentable mistakes I may have made over the years."

She colored a little. "Well, sir, I hope—indeed I *pray*—that on some wondrous occasion in your past you *have* made a mistake of some kind, for that would restore my faith in the fairness of the world!"

He said nothing, putting on his shiny black tall-hat as the groom led a low-necked gray mare from a stall. Lady looked, as Serena had said, as if her interest in life was at the lowest possible ebb. Her floppy ears were stuck out on either side of her head, and her lower lip jutted out slightly. Her tail had not the flicker of motion about it, and when halted she was absolutely motionless, as if to conserve what little strength she had.

"Is she all right?" asked Janine doubtfully, for it seemed it would be a positive crime to mount such a poor creature.

"Perfectly."

"And I'm to perch on that thing on her back?"

"If you are a lady—yes."

"Would you *know* a lady if you met one, Mr. Stuart?"

"I have known many ladies," he replied without glancing at her.

She looked at him. Yes, she believed he'd known a *great* many ladies—

He adjusted the saddle slightly. "Well, let's get on with it—" he began.

"Not here!" she said immediately, glancing around at the waiting grooms. "If you think I'm a performing monkey, you're mistaken. The lesson can begin and end in Calworth Woods."

"Calworth *Woods!* Miss Winterton—"

"No! The woods or nowhere at all; at least if I fall flat on my nose there there'll only be you to see it! Not half of Yorkshire!"

"Very well." He sighed resignedly. "We will begin in Calworth Woods. James? Bring Hal if you please."

Hal proved to be a black horse with four white legs, a white star, and a savage expression in his bright eyes. His neck was arched, he snorted a great deal and was fond of lashing his tail as if it were a whip. Janine was careful to stand well back from him, and she watched doubtfully as Richard swung himself up into the saddle as the fiery horse danced and clattered around in a circle. Riding such a monster surely required a special sort of madness—

"Give Miss Winterton Lady's reins, James," said Richard as he gathered Hal under control.

She took the reins reluctantly, as she began to realize that she must walk the half mile or so to the woods, while Mr. Stuart rode beside her. Gathering her skirts in her other hand, she began to walk, her nose in the air.

He watched for a moment, grinning broadly at her

stiff back. The grooms hid their smiles too as she tugged at Lady, who was determined to go nowhere at all on that sunny afternoon. Richard leaned down and slapped the old mare's rump and she moved at last, going faster than Janine had expected, so that she was forced to hurry to keep up with the animal. Her skirts seemed set on wrapping around her legs as she led the horse out of the stableyard. Richard followed, only a few steps behind her. Then he allowed the chafing Hal to break into a trot, and as he passed her he called out.

"You squeak, Miss Winterton, you squeak!"

After half an hour bump-bumping around the clearing, Janine was convinced that man—or woman—had never been intended to ride horse. Lady was deliberately bumping more than necessary—at least that was the considered conclusion she had come to—and Richard Stuart was determined to make her bounce about as often and as uncomfortably as humanly possible—or equinely possible. She ached in every joint, and one of the ostrich feathers in her hat had fallen forward over her nose so that she felt even more ridiculous than she had before. Walk on. Halt. Walk on. Keep his head up. Heel down. Not that way! That's *possibly* a step in the right direction! Don't let her get away with it, show her who's in command! Wrists down, back straight! As if you *couldn't* have a straight back in these corsets! Was that only four o'clock striking now? It felt more like ten o'clock at night— Oh, blast the nag's neck, all right, all right, I'm keeping it up! She tugged Lady's head up again, and suddenly there was a spark of stubborn life in the old mare. With a strong, swift kick of her back legs, she tipped Janine over her head and into the bracken.

Winded and startled, Janine lay there for a moment without moving.

"Are you all right, Miss Winterton?"

She sat up. Her hair had fallen forward over her face, fragments of broken fern catching in it. The riding habit's full skirts seemed all over the place, and a great deal of her legs were revealed as Richard halted Hal beside her.

"Oh, I'm *perfectly* well," she snapped. "I like lying here like this!"

"You should never tug a horse's mouth, Miss Winterton, as you now know."

"A salutary lesson, Mr. Stuart! You couldn't have taught me better yourself!"

He dismounted, holding out his hand, but she ignored it as she struggled to her feet. He caught her arm suddenly. "Are you sure you're all right?" he asked, searching her face.

"Yes."

"You're very pale."

"So would you be."

"If I were wearing those stays I'm damned sure I would be! You're not to wear them again, do you hear? There's a riding habit over at Talbot Castle, I'll see that you have it to wear."

"Lady Angela's?"

"Yes."

He turned away, catching Lady's trailing reins. She watched him for a moment as she brushed the dirt and leaves from her skirts. The subject of Lady Angela Talbot was obviously not one he intended dwelling on. She picked up her fallen hat and surveyed the crumpled feathers. She'd promised Sir Adam she'd look after the clothes— "Mr. Stuart, do I have a cat in hell's chance of ever being a rider?"

"You and the cat have equal chance of surviving the exercise, Miss Winterton."

"How reassuring."

"Miss Winterton, it is Sir Adam's wish that you learn to ride—"

"Do you always do his bidding so eagerly, Mr. Stuart?"

He looked angrily at her and then remounted. "I think the lesson is at an end, Miss Winterton."

"By all means, *Mr*. Stuart."

From the great height of Hal's back, he looked contemptuously down at her. "I should imagine that my dislike for you is equally matched by yours for me, madam."

She hid the hurt his words dealt out. "Possibly—it would be very difficult to assess which is the greater," she said, meeting his gaze steadily and without showing a thing.

"Why don't you go back to the stage, Miss Winterton, for that is surely where you belong!"

He left her in the clearing, with Lady steadily and rhythmically cropping a patch of grass beside her. She dusted her hat again and watched him as he rode away. Tears stung her eyes and she blinked them away. He was insufferably rude, domineeringly sure of himself, contemptuously condescending and various other unlovable male things—but unreasonably she was more and more drawn to him, and more and more vulnerable to the hurtful things he said—whereas he seemed immune to everything and anything about her.

Chapter 11

She saw nothing more of him that day until dinner, a meal during which Serena barely uttered a word. Only Sir Adam seemed in a talkative mood, for he rattled on as if there were no atmosphere at the table at all, forcing Richard to join in from time to time. Janine spoke when spoken to, not looking at Richard once. She still smarted, both physically and mentally, from her first ride, and her body felt as if it had discovered muscles which should never exist in the first place.

Sir Adam remembered the riding suddenly. "And how did you get on this afternoon, my dear?"

"I fell off."

He threw his head back and laughed. "The more you fall the more you learn to stay on!"

She poked a potato around her gold-rimmed plate, pulling a face. "Is riding compulsory for a Winterton?"

"Compulsory for a *lady*, my dear. Hunting's the thing, and only invalids don't hunt."

"Oh."

"Remember Sir Percy Vere, Janine."

"Who?"

"Sir Percy Vere! Persevere, my dear!"

"Oh." The potato swam through a pool of gravy and lodged against a pile of buttered carrots.

"Cheer up—think of how Peg would have tackled it," said Sir Adam.

She looked at him then. "Peg would not have done anything she didn't want to."

He nodded then. "If it really means all that much to you, then—"

"I'll learn to ride, Grandfather."

There was a strangled sound from Serena at that last word, and Richard glanced warningly at his mother, for her face had suffused to a dull red as she looked across the table at Janine.

Richard cleared his throat. "I shall have to go to York in the morning, Sir Adam."

"Oh? Why's that?"

"There are some good horses to be sold—Lady Hannington's stock. And I have quite a deal of business to attend to, both Calworth and Stuart." He smiled faintly.

"How long will you be away?"

"A week. No more than that."

Sir Adam sighed. "Very well."

Richard's eyebrow flickered very slightly and Janine noticed it in the mirror. He said nothing, but it was obvious that he intended going to York whether it pleased Sir Adam or not, and that the way Sir Adam spoke it was as if he were granting permission.

As Serena and Janine got up at the end of the meal, Richard stood, catching Janine's eye. "Miss Winterton, I sent word to Talbot Castle concerning the riding habit, and it arrived a short while ago. I had it sent up to your room."

"Thank you."

He bowed slightly.

Outside the dining room where the long table seemed dwarfed by the size of the chamber, Janine hurried up to her room. Nothing would have induced her to sit alone in the state room with her aunt.

The riding habit was of dull gold velvet, a garment of great style and dash. Cally had put it out on the bed and was standing admiring it.

"She were a woman of taste, were Lady Angela," she said as Janine ran her hand over the soft velvet.

"It looks a deal more comfortable than Lady Catherine's."

"I remember her wearing it for the Christmas meet last year—no, the year before. Jethro brought her horse out for her and she swept down them steps outside here like a queen, and Master Richard was there to help her mount—"

"Jethro? Your brother works here?"

"Why yes, Miss Janine, he's a groom."

Janine looked at the riding habit again, and then at the maid. "So he can ride?"

"Of course he can ride, he's a grand horseman. Rides Rainbow for Sir Adam at the races."

"Cally, I've just had an idea. Would Jethro teach me to ride?"

"But what about Master Richard?"

"To the Devil with Master Richard Stuart! He's away for a week, a whole week! During that time, if Jethro could teach me—"

Cally grinned. "Jethro'd teach you, Miss Janine, he'd do anything for Peg Oldfield's daughter. But it'd have to be done secret like, for he could get into trouble with Master Richard, or even with Sir Adam."

"Calworth Woods in the evenings."

Cally nodded. "I'll see him later on."

"Will you ask him for me?"

"Yes."

Jethro agreed willingly to help, beginning the following night when Richard had gone, and so it was with a certain sense of satisfaction that Janine went out at dusk to take a walk in the formal gardens. The servants had not lit the lanterns yet and the twilight muted all the colors in the flower beds. A tall hedge of creamy roses filled the night with sweetness, and the sound of the fountains tinkled everywhere. From the open windows of the music room came the sound of the harpsichord again. She knew now that Calworth possessed an excellent orchestra which was permanently in residence, and that it was Serena who liked the harpsichord.

She sat on a stone bench by a tall bed of delphiniums, watching the heavy blooms swaying in the gentle breeze. It was a peaceful moment, a moment to think in. She had been at Calworth for a whole day, long enough to like her grandfather immensely, to dislike her aunt as thoroughly as Serena disliked her, and to be set at sixes and sevens by Richard Stuart. Hardly a moment passed when he did not enter her thoughts one way or another, and the knowledge that she could not help herself was galling in the extreme. There was a great deal of Peg Oldfield in her daughter, she decided wryly, for like Peg, she was capable of choosing quite hopelessly too—

"I tell you, Richard, the old fool is about to acknowledge the girl as his granddaughter, you can feel it coming!"

It was Serena's voice from somewhere beyond the delphiniums and the rose hedge. Janine froze on her seat, not wanting to risk being caught listening, and not wanting to miss anything either.

"Mother, if Sir Adam chooses to acknowledge her, then that is entirely his business."

"But what of Calworth, what of *you*? Until that creature came here you were his heir, heir to everything here! Now—"

"I fail to see what can be done about the inevitable, Mother. Please, calm yourself and accept, as I am."

"I cannot, and nor should you! There—there is a way, though—"

There was an edge of amusement in his laugh. "Very well, what is it?"

"Pay court to her, charm her, and then marry her."

Janine listened in amazement.

There was a long pause before he spoke again. "Mother, I do not *want* to marry her, and nothing— not even possession of Calworth—would induce me to go near her. I love Calworth, I love it very much indeed, but nothing's worth *that!*"

Janine bit her lip miserably. Did he loathe her so much then?

Serena tried again. "She's no Angela, I grant you—"

"No, she isn't. Mother, I do not want to speak about it anymore. I'm fond of you, very fond, but you try my patience at times."

"Oh dear, how like your father you are. Stubborn, clay-headed, proud and above all—*irritating!*"

"It's part of your fatal attraction, is it not? Now then, I intend going inside—shall you come too or remain here in a miff?"

"I'm not in a miff. But I promise you this, Richard. I'll get rid of her, one way or another I'll get rid of her."

"That sounds a little desperate and ill advised."

"I did not mean that I intended *murdering* her!" snapped Serena. "I meant that I'll make sure she's turned out of Calworth!"

"Mother, it could be, you know, that she *is* Henry Winterton's child, in which case she is your niece."

"I don't believe that she is; I don't believe she's got a drop of Winterton blood in a single vein. She's an imposter, an upstart with an eye to the main chance, and I'll not let her get away with it!" Serena paced up and down on the stone flags for a while, her slippers pattering busily. "I can't understand Adam, I can't understand him at all. That wench comes here with a cock-and-bull tale which is virtually impossible to prove, and he makes not even the slightest attempt to verify any of it. We don't even know if Peg Oldfield *had* a daughter, it's as vague and unsatisfactory as that! No, Richard, I cannot allow her to sweep you aside—*something* must be done."

"And you are the one to do it?" he asked, and he still seemed amused by the vehemence in her voice.

"Yes, Richard, I am the one to do it. *I'm* a Winterton, even if Adam appears to have forgotten that he is for the moment."

"Good night, Mother."

"I'm coming in too, it's beginning to get a little cool out here now."

Janine remained motionless on her cold stone seat, her hands clasped miserably in her lap. Suddenly the thought of London and the theater seemed more warming and missed than at any other time. Even the worst days at Miss Tarrant's had not been as dreadful as this one now was. But a promise was a promise, and to decide to leave Calworth after only one day would be weak and a betrayal of her sworn word. Peg wanted her to try, and try she would. And besides—there was her grandfather—

Chapter 12

To her relief, the following day Serena took to her bed with a cold, and with Richard gone to York, meal times were spent alone with her grandfather. She noticed that he allowed her to call him that now without correcting her, and he seemed relaxed and happy in her company. He had a roguish sense of humor, and delighted in telling her tales of life at Calworth during his childhood—tales which she doubted he would have told had Serena been there, as the main protagonist in these fanciful tales was his sister. If he was to be believed, she had gone from one disaster to another throughout her childhood.

"Aye," he said, sitting back after dinner. "And the biggest disaster of all was her marriage to Ander Stuart. Damned Scottish charlatan. Never liked the fellow—how he managed to produce someone like Richard I'll never know."

"Grandfather, Richard was to have been your heir, wasn't he?"

His shrewd eyes rested on her pale face. "There was an unwritten agreement of sorts, yes. Has Serena been cornering you?"

"No."

"She will, she won't be able to help it. A proud, determined and ambitious woman—she always thought the Almighty made a mistake when he made me the son and heir, and not her. Perhaps she's right. So, what she missed herself, she tries now to do through her stepson. Thwarted, frustrated ambition. Aye, but in Richard she's got a man who won't be led, directed or wheedled in any way other than the way *he* wants. He's quite a challenge."

Janine looked curiously at him, wondering what that last statement had meant.

"Enough of all this, let's talk of something more congenial than family affairs. In a few weeks' time is the Calworth Ball. Everyone comes to it, from far and near. It's a masquerade—not masked, but in fancy dress. I love it, I wait each year like a child!" He chuckled as he lit a cigar. "The get-ups which appear, and the people who blossom forth in the wildest of costumes! Even Serena. So, you'll have to think of something startling, they'll expect it particularly of you."

"Why particularly of me?"

"Word's spread that you're Peg Oldfield's daughter; they'll all be agog to see if you've got your mother's flair."

"I'll do my best"—she smiled—"without being too saucy."

"That'll disappoint a lot of them!"

"Is—is word out too that I'm your granddaughter?"

His shrewd pale eyes studied her for a moment. "It may be, I don't know. Rumors will be mushrooming, no doubt it's even said you're the Prince Regent's offspring too by now. It's amazing how the rattle of teacups produces strange distortions. Tea must be an hallucinatory beverage."

"Do you believe I'm your granddaughter?"

He stretched over to touch her cheek very gently.

"Yes," he said softly, "I believe that you are. You belong at Calworth, Janine, and your fresh presence has brightened up my life a very great deal in so short a time. Serena'll come round in the end, don't you fret, and as for Richard—well, I can't tell what he's thinking most of the time anyway, and he don't have a great deal to say. Don't let him affect you so."

She stared, blushing suddenly. Had she been that obvious?

As if he knew what she was thinking, he shook his head. "I'm an old man, but I don't miss a thing. And you, sweetheart, I feel I know so well already that I can *sense* how you feel. It's not often in my life that I've experienced such closeness with another human being. The only other time was with Henry—your father. We lost that closeness in the end, but it was good while it was there. And now, unexpectedly and delightfully, I can experience it again with you, Janine. Now then, if you don't get off for that riding lesson with Jethro Arkwright, there'll be hardly any light left."

She stood, smiling at him. "Is there anything you don't know about?"

"I'm the spider, and this is my web," he said, waving a hand around. "Any spider worth his salt makes sure he knows what's caught in the web, eh?"

In Lady Angela's riding habit, it was far more comfortable on Lady's back, and with the more patient, placid Jethro to instruct her, she felt infinitely more confident. Around and around the clearing she went, watched by Cally who sat on a small picnic basket, her cloak pulled tightly around her for there was a strong breeze which rustled through the trees. The chimes on the pagoda drifted with each breath, and the scents of strange blossoms from the variety of ornamental trees.

"That's it, Miss Janine, you're doing grand now. Keep a straight back and you'll sit firmer. Grand. Now then, bring her up to a smarter trot. Steady now, you've got her in the palm of your hand."

Lady was surprisingly amenable today, obeying each command willingly. As darkness was falling, Janine managed her first canter. It was a little terrifying with the trees looming all around, their leaves bending and twisting in the wind, but at the same time it was exhilarating.

"There now." Jethro grinned, catching the reins as she halted at last. "What d'you reckon to riding now, eh?"

"Ee, it's grand," she said.

He laughed. "Reckon you'll do, Miss Janine. Come th'end of the week you'll be riding like you was born to it."

"If my limbs and tail stand up to it."

"We put liniment on horses, reckon I don't know what young ladies put on," he said, grinning again as he patted Lady's nose. "She's a grand old girl, eh?"

Janine nodded, pulling one of the mare's floppy ears.

"Too old for a lot of riding, we'll have to pick out something else come the end of the week."

"Nothing too spirited!"

"It won't breathe fire and smoke, if that's what you mean."

"That's exactly what I mean. Oh, Cally, do you think that champagne is still cold?"

"I put enough ice around it from the ice-house," said the maid, opening the hamper.

Janine handed the bottle to Jethro for him to open. "I somehow had a feeling that I'd be wanting to celebrate a little tonight. Contrary to Mr. Richard Stuart, I am *not* a dunce without the first notion of how to remain upright on a horse!" she said, laughing as the cork popped.

"*Three* glasses, Miss Janine?" asked Cally uncertainly.

"Yes. One each."

"*We're* to drink Sir Adam's champagne?"

"Yes. Oh, come on, I'm dying to taste it!"

"If there were four glasses then I could join you," said another voice from the edge of the clearing, and Cally squeaked as she whirled around.

A gentleman stood there, holding the reins of a white horse. He was tall, with almost golden hair, and he wore a coat which shone blue in the light from the lantern Jethro had brought.

"Who is it?" whispered Janine.

"Lord Talbot," said Cally, dropping a belated curtsey as he tethered his horse and came across the clearing toward them.

He bowed to Janine. "Miss Winterton?"

"My lord." She curtseyed.

His eyes moved momentarily to Cally and Jethro, and without a word they moved away to a discreet distance, taking Lady with them. "Curiosity dragged me from my lair to see the new addition to Calworth's household. I see that my sister's riding habit has found itself yet another beautiful owner."

"You flatter me, sir."

"No, I don't." He picked up the bottle of champagne which was on the grass where Jethro had put it. "A celebration?"

"My first successful ride."

"A worthy cause indeed. I refuse to be excluded."

"Then you must join us, but I do not accept the company of those who do not introduce themselves properly."

He smiled, his lean face lightening. "Mark Talbot, your servant."

"Janine Winterton."

He took her hand and raised it to his lips. "David Wolfe said you were quite the most beautiful woman he had ever seen, and now I can quite agree with him."

Her smile faded. "*Lord* Wolfe?"

"Yes."

"I would hardly take a recommendation from him concerning anything whatsoever, my lord."

"I think he knows he's queered his pitch, Miss Winterton. I've seldom seen him more sunk in gloom and despondency."

"Let him sink."

He picked up one of the glasses. "Now it seems to me," he said, changing the subject, "that either you and I must share a glass, or your servants must."

"They will not mind sharing," she said quickly, uncertain of him. She could not read him at all, but her curiosity made her stay to talk with him.

He took the bottle to Jethro and poured a brimming glass. Cally's eyes were like saucers again and she almost forgot her curtsey, but Jethro jogged her arm.

He then poured some for Janine. "Forgive me mentioning Wolfe," he said, looking at her, "but I thought I should as he's by way of being a cousin—removed a few times, etcetera, etcetera. I *do* know him and he does come to stay at Talbot occasionally. It seemed only fair and right that I should inform you. Well now, that toast. To your first successful ride."

She raised her glass and touched it against his. Since his mention of David Wolfe she had not smiled, but now that she looked into his green eyes she suddenly smiled again. "My ride."

"I came to see Richard, but with the sneaking hope I might come face to face with you. You're very like your mother—I saw her perform a few times."

"News travels. What have you heard about me, my lord?"

"That you've horns and a forked tail and keep a pitchfork under your pillow. Apart from that, that you're Peg Oldfield's daughter and—more to the point—that Henry Winterton was your father."

"The last two are correct, but as to the first—"

"Well, maybe I exaggerated about the pitchfork!"

She drank some of the ice-cold champagne, savoring the fizzy, sparkling taste. "It was kind of you to let me have you sister's riding habit."

"Kind? I didn't mind at all—instinct told me you'd be more than worthy of it."

"You have a way with words, my lord."

"I'm trying to charm you."

"And I'm beginning to feel flattered again. I'm also beginning to feel that I've lingered out here with you far too long and that it's not acceptable conduct on my part."

"It isn't, but I wasn't going to remind you of such an *ennui*-inducing formality."

She smiled. "I'm glad to have met you, my lord."

His green eyes met hers for a moment, and then he bowed, returning to his horse. "Good night, Miss Winterton. We'll meet again in a week's time."

"A week's time?"

"I'm invited to dine here, and now I find that I'm more than looking forward to the occasion." He tapped his top hat on his golden hair and turned the horse.

She watched him ride away into the darkness, and then turned to where Cally and Jethro still waited. Cally crossed toward her, clutching the little hamper and the glass. "We'd best be getting in, Miss Janine."

"I know, but let's just finish the champagne, mm?"

"I'll be tipsy."

"No, you won't. Come on, Jethro, there's plenty here."

Cally sipped it again and closed her eyes. "Oh, it's a grand taste, all diamonds and lace. All music and fancy balls, carriages and things like that."

Janine looked at the glass. It was all those things, but it was also theater, first nights, curtain calls and celebrations at Cane's Tea Rooms.

"He's very handsome, isn't he, Miss Janine?" said Cally suddenly.

"Who?"

"Why Lord Talbot, of course. He makes my toes all curl up."

"Cally!" Jethro scowled at her. "That's not suitable talk! You've had enough of that there champagne."

Janine protested. "The amount of champagne she's had can't have affected her at all."

Cally beamed. "It hasn't. But I had two big glasses of Mrs. Bentley's elderberry wine afore coming out and I feel quite light-headed. And I'm enjoying it, Jethro Arkwright, so there!"

Chapter 13

A week later, on the day of Richard's return from York, Janine dressed with great care and attention for dinner. Her grandfather had said that it would be a formal dinner party, and so she laid out her mother's grand gowns on the bed to decide which one to wear.

"What do you think, Cally?"

"That blue gauzy one's the one I like, it goes with your eyes."

"It's very—well, revealing."

"But that's the thing, isn't it? I've seen some ladies come here with dresses you can see right through, and some as damps their underskirts to make them cling. And this one *is* very pretty. I know one thing, *I'd* like to sit opposite Lord Talbot wearing it!"

Janine smiled at her. "Don't let Jethro hear you say that. And speaking of Jethro, don't you think I've come on this week? Last night he actually brought me another horse for the first time. It was *huge*, it felt like being up on the first floor."

Cally laughed. "Gemine's not *that* big!"

"Big enough. Anyway, thanks to your brother I

won't have to put up with Mr. Hoity-Toity's company."

"If 'putting up's' the right word," said Cally, glancing at her.

"What do you mean by that?"

"Well, it's just—oh, nothing."

"Cally!"

"All right, I was just going to say—begging your pardon afore I say it—that you wouldn't get so mad with him if'n you weren't—well—*interested*. Now you're all angry and I'm sorry."

"It's all right, Cally, I'm not angry." Janine sat down on the bed among the profusion of costly gowns. "You're right, and I only wish you weren't. He can't stand the sight of me or the sound of my name. Damn him, damn *all* of them."

"Console yourself. I would." Cally picked up the blue gown and shook it out. "There's more handsome fish in the sea, fish with golden hair and big, soulful green eyes."

Janine lay back on the bed laughing. "Oh, Cally, I don't know what I'd do without you to cheer me up sometimes."

The door opened suddenly, and Serena stood there. Cally's smile vanished and she scuttled from the room without a word, leaving Janine to sit up.

Serena closed the door slowly. Her red hair was hidden beneath a green silk turban around which strings of pearls were looped, and her flowing tunic gown had a train which dragged the floor behind her.

"I think it time a few things were said between us, missy," she said, clasping her hands purposefully before her.

Janine stood. "*I* have nothing to say, my lady."

"I have. I do not believe you are my niece, and it would take a great deal to ever convince me you are other than an opportunist. Calworth will go to my stepson, and I regard it as my bounden duty to expose you for what you are—a stage-born strumpet."

Janine looked into her aunt's flushed, angry face. "I understand how you feel about me, my lady, believe me I do. But you are wrong, for I *am* your niece. I don't want to deprive Richard Stuart of anything, indeed he is welcome to Calworth. I assure you that I remain here now simply and solely because I love my grandfather."

"How sweet. I can see well enough how you've inveigled your way into Adam's fool heart— That trick with Catherine's riding habit was a stroke of genius worthy of Peg Oldfield herself. I am not fooled by your innocent air, missy. I leave you with this warning. I intend defeating you, so you may keep glancing over your lily-white shoulder from this moment on."

Janine raised her chin. "One day you will know how wrong you are right now, my lady. Now, if you please. Get *out!*"

Serena blinked at the force of the last word, looking taken aback. But Janine learned her lessons well, and Miss Tarrant again would have been proud of her former pupil. She went to the door and held it open without another word. Serena stood uncertainly for a moment and then turned on her heel, sweeping past in a rustle of pale green silk, diamonds and lavender water.

Janine closed the door weakly. When Cally returned a few minutes later, she found her mistress lying on the bed weeping.

"Oh, Miss Janine," cried the maid, hurrying to her.

"I'm all right." Janine sniffed, sitting up and dabbing her eyes. "I don't know whether it's self-pity or downright fury. I'm all right now." She took a deep breath. "I'll warrant my eyes are red and puffy now."

"No, they're not, but don't rub them, whatever you do!" warned Cally.

"I'm not. Oh dear, I've got hardly any time to get ready now!"

"We'll manage, don't you worry. Oh, that Lady Serena!"

"It's not her fault, Cally. She really does think I'm lying about everything. I can't blame her, not if I'm honest with myself. At least she's told me to my face, I think a little more of her for that. Now then—the blue gauze?"

"The blue gauze."

"Oh, I don't really want to face anyone now, especially not my aunt or her stepson."

"Think of Lord Talbot. *He'd* make any evening worthwhile."

Janine smiled in spite of herself. "Oh, Cally, you almost deserve to snap him up."

"I don't, you know. I'm handfast to Tom Mayhew, I shouldn't be taking side looks at anyone let alone a lord! Tom'd flay me one if he knew, that's why Jethro gets so annoyed with me. But a girl can't help letting her eye rove, can she? So long as it's just the eye and nothing else!"

"I didn't even know you were engaged."

"Oh, yes, me and Tom's walked out for years and years. We could've married a long time back, but somehow it's just rambled on. Anyway, thanks to Master Richard he's getting the tenancy of Edge Farm soon, so I reckon I'll be up that aisle then. Now then, let's get your hair all done up—"

The dinner was not as unendurable as Janine had expected. Serena said little, behaving as she had done before her confrontation with her niece. Sir Adam was in beatific mood, and he found a ready echo in Mark Talbot. Richard put himself out for once and proved to be good and amusing company, with anecdotes of the Highland region of his birth which made even his stepmother smile—but Janine guessed that a smile from Serena in her present mood probably pained her as much as the drawing of a back tooth!

A week at Calworth without Richard Stuart to distract her had proved one salutary thing to her—she was in love with him. When Lord Talbot and her grandfather complimented her on her appearance and he had said little or nothing, it had hurt her. It would have cost him nothing to murmur *something*, but there was not so much as an approving glance. The attention she received from Mark Talbot made Richard's *lack* of attention all the more painful and obvious. She resigned herself to the fact that he loathed her, that everything about her was a complete anathema to him and that there was absolutely no hope of his attitude ever changing.

As the liqueurs were served, Mark looked across at her. "I've been plucking up my dismal courage all evening to beg a favor of you, Miss Winterton."

"Of me?"

"Yes. A ride with you tomorrow morning."

Richard looked at her then, his dark eyes pensive.

"I would like that, my lord. Thank you." She was conscious of Richard's continuing perusal.

Mark stood. "And now, I shall rely upon your good humor, Sir Adam, for I am about to presume yet again. Miss Winterton, will you walk with me in the gardens? It's such a lovely evening and—"

"I should like that too, my lord," she said, smiling at him.

"Go on then," said Sir Adam. "I'm not done with my liqueur yet. I *do* like a couple of glasses of liqueur to round off a fine meal."

Outside in the warm evening air, Mark drew her hand through his arm. "You'd been crying before you came down this evening, hadn't you?" he asked suddenly.

"No."

"Don't fib, Miss Winterton, I'm too sharp to miss such a thing, especially where you're concerned." He stopped, putting his other hand over hers. "Is something wrong?"

"No. Not really."

"I'm also wily enough to recognize a noncommittal answer when I hear it. And to recognize an Atmosphere. Richard was extraordinarily taciturn at one point tonight, before he used his undoubted skill as a *raconteur*, and Lady Serena was *fiercely* silent."

"She's fiercely everything. Like a dragon."

He smiled. "You threaten her stepson, don't you know! Where Richard's concerned she's more than a dragon, she's a positive tiger! And there's little need, for he's more than capable of looking after himself. As my headstrong, willful sister found, to her cost."

"In what way?"

"Angela was perhaps the most determined woman I've ever known. Nothing was to stand in her way. She was an aristocrat of the first order, and determined to be that every moment of her life. And, by God, she was. She even frightened *me* at times. She set her cap at Richard Stuart from the moment she saw him. There was something aloof and un-get-at-able about him, if you know what I mean. It drove Angela to distraction, and she used every trick she knew to win him."

"And succeeded?"

"I don't know, and that's the truth."

"But, if they were betrothed—"

"I don't know that they were. Oh, yes, I suppose they were, but it never had a permanent ring about it to me. *She* seemed full of her success, prattling about it endlessly until I was praying for the wedding day so that Calworth could listen for a change."

"Why didn't you think it was permanent? Surely—"

"I think he may have realized one day exactly how fearsome and *ancien régime* she was. My sister would have flourished in France in the early years of the last century, Miss Winterton, but in England, and with a *Scot*—I think the mixture would have proved disastrous. Fur would have flown the first moment he put her in her place—or at least, attempted to."

"I believe, my lord, that if Mr. Stuart attempted then he would succeed. He is capable of putting anyone in their place."

He glanced at her. "That came from the heart."

She smiled, but did not reply.

"I look forward to that ride," he said suddenly.

"If I say that I do too, you won't—?"

"Think you forward and therefore place odious hopes upon it?" He put her fingers to his lips. "I will not think the first, and will endeavor not to ever even *dream* of the second. If ever life at Calworth becomes unbearable, Miss Janine Winterton, you are to come to seek solace on my waiting shoulder, promise me that. And now, as being alone in the moonlight with such a vision of loveliness is doing my constitution little good, and can be doing Sir Adam's peace of mind little good either, I think we should take ourselves back inside."

They walked slowly around the fragrant flower beds, and she looked up at the great house which was ablaze with lights in every window. He watched her pensive expression. "Are you happy here?" he asked.

"No."

"But you will stay?"

"I don't know. I don't think so." Being asked outright like that had prompted a decision. She *didn't* want to stay, not even for love of her grandfather. There were few moments of life at Calworth which she really and truly enjoyed, and Serena's attitude was not the cause of her unhappiness, it all came back to Richard Stuart.

Mark halted, turning her to face him. "Allow me time to persuade you how lovable we are," he said with a smile. "You'll be here for the Calworth Ball, won't you?"

"Until then, yes." But for how much longer could she endure her feelings?

Chapter 14

The night was hot and close, and Janine lay on her bed
with only a light sheet, but even that seemed stifling.
She got up and brushed her hair, but whatever she did,
she felt uncomfortably warm. There must be thunder
near— She went to the window and looked out. The
lanterns in the trees had been extinguished now and
everything was dark, there was no moon anymore and
clouds hid the stars. The wind had dropped to nothing.
It was silent and eery out there, and she shivered. Outside it was cooler, and suddenly she turned and took a
light mantle from the wardrobe and slipped her feet
into slippers.

The house was deserted, none of the doors had their
usual footmen sentries and there was no one at the
main doors to fling them open for her. She just walked
out and down the flight of wide steps to the driveway.
She hurried well away from the house, for somehow it
was the house itself which was oppressing her tonight.
She couldn't stay here. Having come to the decision,
she was restless. If it were not for her grandfather—

She had kept her promise to her mother, Peg would know and accept that.

She halted, looking up at the dark skies. Peg had joked that the place reserved for her was a little more hot than the cool, celestial heavens! She'd even had a song about it! She'd painted her face as gaudily as she could, worn a gown which dipped seemingly to her waist, made of the filmiest fabric which revealed rather too much. It was Peg's sauciest song, and one of her most popular. Janine sat on the edge of a lily pool, remembering.

"I'm too wicked for them up there, I make 'em blush and stare!" Most of the words had been drowned by the cheering, clapping audience, for this song had frequently finished Peg's performance. She stood suddenly, swaggering along the pathway with her hands on her hips as Peg had done. She sang the words under her breath, for the night was too silent and listening, but she did not stint her performance in any other way. As she finished she took an imaginery bow, acknowledging the roars of the nonexistent audience, blowing kisses and picking up the bouquets.

A single pair of hands suddenly clapped, and she froze.

"How vastly entertaining, Miss Winterton," said Richard, coming forward from the shadows by a statue, still clapping.

Her face was so red she felt it must be like a beacon. "I did not know you were there, Mr. Stuart."

"Obviously."

"It would have become you more, sir, had you intimated that you were present."

"I was too entertained by your performance."

"And it's easier to mock than to be thoughtful for a change, isn't it?"

"You seem to be under the illusion that I give you a great deal of my thoughts, Miss Winterton."

"Because you do, just as your mother—correction, your *step*mother—does. You both wonder about your position here if my grandfather makes me publicly his heir."

"And how would you know *what* I thought about anything?"

"I don't, it's an educated guess."

"Totally incorrect. Your advent, Miss Winterton, matters not one jot to me."

"Even losing Calworth?"

His eyes flickered. "Calworth was never mine to lose."

"Wasn't it? I was under the impression that you were his heir until I came. Perhaps that is why you've been lavishing so much care and attention upon your inheritance."

"I care for Calworth, that's true. But my reasons for the hard work I've put in here have nothing to do with any expectancy of gaining it myself one day."

"I believe the expression goes—'Pull the other one, it has bells'!"

He smiled faintly. "How quaint. Anyway, the question is academic, is it not? You are Sir Adam's granddaugher."

"You believe me then?"

"I have never said I did not."

"Lady Serena most definitely has."

"That is up to her. I believe you are Henry Winterton's daughter, although from which side of the blanket is surely another matter."

She raised her hand furiously at the insult to her mother, but he caught her wrist in a firm grip. "I would not advise it, Miss Winterton, for I'm boor enough to strike you back."

"That I believe!" she cried, "for more of a boor I've never met in my life! You are surely a poor example of your race, sirrah! Taking refuge in making my life miserable!"

"I've done nothing of the sort. I've been most careful to stay *out* of your way completely! One day's business was stretched to a week in York!"

"My heart bleeds! I pray the bed had bugs, the wine was sour and the food gave you a bellyache! And that the carriage axle broke six times over and each time you were set in a ditch!"

He released her hand. "The Almighty obviously pays scant attention to your prayers. Perhaps I should not have said what I did, forgive me."

"You still think it, though, so your apology is empty."

"I must think it, for I cannot imagine a man like Henry Winterton marrying anyone unless she was wealthy, titled and landed. Peg Oldfield was none of these things. Wondrously alluring, maybe, vivacious, infectiously good company. But not marriage material for Henry Winterton. He was no Mark Talbot."

"And what might that mean?" she demanded, sensing the barb.

"Come now, his interest tonight was obvious and unsubtle."

"And what business is it of yours?"

"None whatsoever."

"Then why mention it?"

"Because I was pondering how well you are doing there. Not only will you get Calworth, but maybe Talbot as well, and a nice, ancient, respected title. If you could, no doubt you'd pat your own back."

"I certainly wouldn't ask you to do it for me!" she snapped. "And speaking of titles, perhaps I have one already. If I'm Sir Adam's granddaughter, his direct heir, then surely *his* title comes to me! And as for wanting Calworth—well, I don't! Since coming here, I've been more miserable than at any other time in my life. Only my grandfather and Lord Talbot have shown me any remote kindness, except for those among the servants whom I've come to know—"

"Ah, the common touch."

"Even some sovereigns had that, but obviously no Scottish ones! I stay here now only because of my grandfather and for no other reason whatsoever."

A sudden breath of wind disturbed the nearby trees, bringing a coolness which held the promise of coming rain, and Janine's mantle lifted and her hair dragged across her face.

"You make it sound as if your sojourn at Calworth is in imminent danger of coming to an end, Miss Winterton," he said.

"If it is I would not tell you, sir. In fact, I'd say nothing whatsoever, simply to annoy you!"

"I believe you."

"You deserve little else."

"As I deserved not to be informed about your riding lessons?"

"Yes—besides, you were not here to inform."

"Would you have done had I been here?"

"No. Your conduct over the first lesson was proof enough to me that you dislike me, dislike having to teach me, dislike even having to speak to me unless it's to be rude and arrogant."

"You seem very certain of what *I* feel, Miss Winterton—maybe you are wrong."

"Maybe capons will pluck themselves this year."

The wind strengthened, ruffling his hair and making his white shirt flap against his arms. "A quaint turn of phrase, Miss Winterton, and a quaintly sharp tongue—which I dislike in a woman."

"No doubt in Scotland I would be turned out with the other domesticated animals in the yard!" she said sourly.

"Perhaps, but you are unfortunately not in Scotland,

you are here at Calworth. You may speak like a lady,
look like one and—for the most part—behave like one,
but there are times when your conduct leaves much to
be desired. Fraternizing with servants is one prime example."

"No doubt Lady Angela would never have so con-
descended," she snapped furiously.

He paused, looking beyond her for a moment. "No,
she would not. She was an aristocrat to her very fingertips."

"Whereas I am an actress' daughter?" she said
softly. "And what are you, sirrah, but a parvenu with
notions of being master of Calworth?" She walked past
him, her chin up, just as the first raindrops pattered
over the gardens. Her steps quickened, but by the time
she reached the shelter of the house, it was not just the
rain which dampened her cheeks.

Chapter 15

The rain had gone by the next morning, but the skies were still lowering as Janine emerged at last for her ride. The butler had informed her that Lord Talbot was in the stableyard talking with Richard, and so it was with great unease that she walked down the front steps to the driveway. Angela's riding habit was full, and she had to gather it up a great deal in order to walk, but she'd practiced for hours in her room and now she had the knack of it very well. A dark brown beaver hat was perched on the side of her head, a bouncy feather curling from its golden band. She pulled on her gloves, praying that when she mounted Gemine and began her ride, she would do nothing foolish in front of Richard.

Mark's white horse stood with Gemine, a groom waiting patiently with the reins, and beyond them she saw Mark and Richard by the stall where the mare and foal were.

Mark turned immediately as he heard her, but Richard finished his sentence before doing so. They both watched her as she walked across the damp cobbles where puddles lurked in every crevice.

Mark kissed his fingertips. "*Superbe!*" he said with a smile.

"Why thank you, sir," she replied, with a deep curtsey.

Richard said nothing, but merely looked at her. He had not been at the breakfast table that morning, and this was the first time she had seen him since the night before.

"Good morning, Mr. Stuart," she said pointedly.

He inclined his head. "Good morning, Miss Winterton."

She felt like pulling a face at him, but restrained the urge which was almost too strong for safety. She smiled at Mark instead. "Shall we go, then? I don't like the look of the weather."

He offered her his arm and they walked across to the horses. She mounted Gemine elegantly—if mounting side saddle was ever elegant—and she knew that Richard was watching her every move. He had crossed the yard too and now held Gemine's reins as she arranged her skirts. He still held them for a moment as Mark began to ride out of the yard.

"I trust you *are* competent enough to ride Gemine, Miss Winterton."

"I am."

"Nonetheless—"

"If I *did* take a fall, Mr. Stuart, at least this time I would be with a gentleman who would be concerned about my welfare!"

"Undoubtedly, for Talbot has a decided penchant for dainty ankles and a flurry of underskirts."

"Crude as well as boorish this morning, Mr. Stuart?" she asked, taking up the reins and turning Gemine away from him.

The hooves clattered on the cobbles as she rode to where Mark waited, and in a moment they were riding down the driveway toward Calworth Woods.

The air was cool and damp beneath the trees, and the soft ground muffled the sound of the horses' hooves, but as Janine caught sight of the pagoda through the glades, she reined in.

"Can we look at the pagoda?"

"Why not?" he said, turning his restless horse.

Close to, the pagoda seemed to stretch to the skies, its gold-tipped roofs shining brightly against the dull skies where the clouds were scudding past so swiftly. The chimes jingled constantly against the red and purple paintwork, and around its base there was a Chinese garden like the one painted on the walls of her room.

"Angela liked it here so much she decided to have her bedroom painted to look like it," he said as if he heard her thoughts. "Even the one she was to occupy at Calworth."

"I know, I love it."

"Chinoiserie was a rage with her—I began to fear she would want rice with every meal—but luckily I was spared that, she liked her food too much!"

She smiled at him. "You must miss her a lot."

"I do—if only because the castle's so quiet now. She was a bright star, burning fiercely for a short while and leaving us all somewhat breathless by the suddenness of her going."

She looked around the little garden with its tumbling waterfalls and little bridges where the azaleas sparkled with moisture. Golden fish darted in the pools, vanishing beneath the broad lily leaves like molten metal. Had Richard loved the dazzling Angela very deeply? How could any living woman compete with a ghost of such style and vigor? Not that such a competition was ever likely to involve Janine Winterton—

"Shall we ride on?" asked Mark.

"Yes."

"The moors or the moors?" He laughed.

"Oh, the moors, of course!"

On the open heath the clouds seemed closer, almost as if she could reach up and touch them. The heather was wet and fresh, as was the gorse, the colors looking washed and clean. The moors stretched as far as the eye could see, clear and distinct, without a heat haze or mist to distort the distance or depth of the countryside. Great crags of rock topped each rise in the land, the scree falling grayly until it mingled with the wiry grass and the heather.

After they had ridden for some time, Mark reined in, pointing at a standing stone to their right. "The moment you pass that stone you are on Talbot land. It's called the Dog Stone."

"Why?"

"My family's emblem is a Talbot hound, and in times gone by the Talbots and Wintertons were less than friendly. One of your forebears contemptuously referred to the boundary as where man ended and dogs began, and so it's been the Dog Stone ever since."

"The remark sounds more like one a Stuart would make," she said.

He smiled. "Richard's a dour Scot."

"I would describe him otherwise."

"So it seems."

"Help me down, will you? Please?"

He dismounted and reached up to her, and she slid to the heather. "It's so very wide and open up here, isn't it?" she said. "And there's so much of it."

"Too wide and open for a city girl?"

"I think so."

"Or is it the atmosphere at Calworth which makes you feel that way?"

"I don't know. I *do* miss the theater, though. I missed it when I was at that awful academy, and I miss it still. I'm too much my mother's daughter."

She walked toward a rock, leaning against it, her

riding crop tapping against it. Whichever way she looked from this point, there was not a house to be seen, except the distant roof of Calworth, and on this gray day the scene was desolate.

He came closer, leaning one hand on the rock and looking into her face. Then he bent his head and kissed her very gently on the lips. "When I look at you and see you so sad, I cannot help myself, Janine," he said softly, "which is poor excuse for poor behavior on my part."

At that moment a hawk swooped low from the ridge behind them, soaring above the heads of the two horses and frightening Gemine, who reared, turning in a moment before Mark could reach her trailing reins. Her hooves drummed on the moor as she set off back toward Calworth, but Mark's horse remained where it was, reacting only by tossing its head and snorting.

"Damn that hawk!" said Mark, watching the frightened horse until it passed beyond the fall of the land. "We'd best get back as quickly as we can, they'll think you've been hurt—"

She let him lift her onto the saddle of his horse, and he mounted behind her, an arm lightly around her waist. They rode slowly back the way they had come, and as they reached the brow of the hill opposite Calworth, he reined in, looking at her.

"May I call upon you again, Janine? Or have I made myself *persona non grata?*"

She put her hand over his. "I like you, Mark Talbot, I like you very much—as a friend. If you know and accept that, then I would love to see you again."

His green eyes searched her face for a moment. "That's me in my place," he said, smiling. "For the time being, anyway—for I shall not give up all hope that you will one day fall into my arms."

"I do not think that I ever will, you know," she said seriously.

"There is someone else?"

"Yes."

"Who?"

"That is not your concern, Mark."

He looked beyond her suddenly, his smile fading. "Good God! They've got the hounds out looking for you!"

She stared as the four horsemen rode up from the valley, and in the lead she recognized Richard. The hounds bayed as they strained at their leashes, their noses to the trail, and as they reached the white horse, they broke into excited noise, rushing and straining all the more, their tails wagging.

Richard reined in, his face angry. "I presume," he said tartly, "that you have come to no harm, Miss Winterton!"

"A hawk frightened Gemine, but I wasn't on her—"

"Indeed!" he snapped, waving the horsemen and hounds away. "And did it not occur to you that your riderless horse might cause some concern?"

Mark stiffened at Richard's tone. "The thought had crossed my mind, Richard!" he said, his voice cold.

"Not swiftly enough, my lord," returned Richard, "for I did not perceive any undue haste in your return!"

"It is still a little dramatic to call out hounds, surely?" said Mark.

"I agree, but then mine was not the order. Your grandfather, Miss Winterton, was in the stableyard when Gemine returned, and he is very frightened and fearful for your safety. Nothing would suffice but going out with the hounds. While you dally across the moors at snail's pace, he is frantic with worry!"

She stared at him. "Is he all right?"

"He's an old, frail man, Miss Winterton. He's as well as you would expect under the circumstances!"

Mark dismounted and helped her down, and one of

the horsemen led Gemine across. Then Mark caught Richard's bridle. "You are straining the bounds of friendship, Richard," he said. "*I* don't deserve the edge of your tongue, and Miss Winterton certainly does not!"

"If you are not capable of escorting one woman on a short ride in reasonable weather, my lord, perhaps we should consider the friendship strained indeed!" snapped Richard. "Now, Miss Winterton, get yourself back to Calworth and allay your grandfather's fears!"

The man helped her to mount, and without another word she urged Gemine away, her face crimson with anger and embarrassment.

Mark still held the bridle. "One more word, Stuart, and I'll call you out!"

"Call me out for being justifiably angry at the distress caused to an old man I think highly of? I think not, my lord!"

Mark dropped his hand, and Richard turned his horse away, following in Janine's wake.

Mark watched until all the horsemen from Calworth had vanished from view in the valley, and then he mounted again. He looked back at Calworth for a moment before beginning his journey to Talbot Castle.

Chapter 16

"Grandfather?"

He turned from contemplating the Van Dyke above the mantelpiece in the state room. "I saw that you were safe, my dear."

His hands were shaking as she clasped them. "I'm sorry," she whispered.

"An old fool's momentary panic is hardly your fault, sweetheart," he murmured, patting her hands gently. "I panicked because for a while it was like—like it was when Henry died. Oh, I know I was here in England and he was somewhere on the ocean, but there was a terrible storm here. It came up suddenly high on the moors and shook and screamed around Calworth for a day and a night. All that time I had a sense of foreboding, I *knew* he'd gone from me— A month later I heard. There were a few survivors from the loss of the *Christabelle*—she'd been lost at the very time of the storm. Then today, just for that sudden moment, that foreboding was there again. Janine, if ever I could have doubted your birthright, I cannot doubt it now. The thought that maybe I'd lost you made my feelings on that point only too clear." He hugged her tightly, his cheek against her hair.

"Richard's very angry with me," she said after a long moment. "I think he'd horsewhip me, given his way."

He smiled, staring beyond her at the crimson saloon. "Would he, be damned? I think my fit of the vapors has caused more trouble than a cat in a pigeon loft. Is—is Mark still among Calworth's friends?"

"Just about."

"Richard?"

"Yes."

"Richard Stuart may not really be my nephew, Janine, but there is a bond between us. My dodderings affect him, just as it affects me that I must— Well, that's for another day, not just *à ce moment*. Well, off with you to change, you look hot, flustered and uncomfortable in that riding habit."

"I feel it."

She left him by the huge mantelpiece, glancing back as she reached the doors. He looked small and frail, almost lost among the grand and priceless treasures of that rich room.

In her room she found not Cally, but Richard. He still held his riding crop and his top hat had been tossed carelessly on her bed. She closed the door and turned to face him. "Yes?" She stood stiffly, waiting for him to speak.

"You came here of your own volition, madam, intent upon being recognized as a Winterton. Well, you've succeeded, and by God it's time you began behaving as a Winterton would behave, not as if you were more used to the life of a *demi-mondaine*."

"I beg your pardon?" she said frostily, every nerve quivering.

"You heard me."

"I am waiting for an explanation of that great insult, sirrah."

"You will be heiress to all this." He waved his arm at the house. "And upon your shoulders the Winterton name will be carried. So far, I have found you to have hobnobbed with servants, walked alone in the gardens at night in your shift, spent time alone with Talbot on at least three occasions—the last of which was today. *I* would not have permitted you to take that ride at all!"

"Oh, *wouldn't* you! And what earthly business is it of yours? You are insufferable, quite the most rude and conceited *person* I've ever encountered. How *dare* you suggest that my conduct is forward and shameless, how *dare* you! It's already been my dubious pleasure to throw my aunt out of this room, and now I do the same to you! Get out, Richard Stuart, and if you have nothing better to do than insult me with every word you utter, you'd be better employed closing your mouth entirely!" She opened the door.

Without another glance at her, he strode from the room, and she slammed the door behind him with such force she thought she might have broken the handle. She shook from head to toe, snatching up the cushion again and flinging it with all her might at the wall. Then she picked it up and repeated the exercise.

It was a short while later, when she had calmed down a little, that her glance fell on his excellent top hat on the bed. She glared at it, thinking of stamping on it for a moment, but then another notion entered her head. Snatching it up, she left the room, hurrying past the silent footmen at their places, who must surely have heard every word of her altercation with Richard, down the curving black marble staircase into the hall and out on to the steps. The gardeners were working busily at the flower beds and hardly looked up as she went more sedately down the steps to the driveway, and then into the formal gardens. She glanced around until she saw the statue she wanted. Scaramouche posed there, every inch the boastful braggart. Looking around carefully, she went to the statue, climbing up like an urchin scrumping apples. Carefully, she put the top hat on the statue's head and then lowered herself again. No one seemed to have noticed what she'd done, and she strolled casually between the flower beds and pools, glancing back at the statue from time to time. The black, shiny top hat was quite plain. "MacScaramouche!" she said to herself, turning to go back inside.

Cally was in her room, and looked in surprise as Janine beckoned her out into the corridor. From a window Janine pointed at the top hat.

"Oh, Miss Janine!" gasped the maid.

"I'd like to punch him on the nose really, but this gesture will have to do."

Cally's eyes were huge as she looked at her mistress' face. "He'll be right mad about this."

"I trust it gives him apoplexy. Oh, look, he's out there now."

They watched as Richard came from the far end of the garden, calling the head gardener to point out something in one of the flower beds. The gardener nodded, gesturing about something as he spoke, but suddenly his arms were still as he stared up at the statue. Richard followed his gaze and the two of them looked up at the top hat. Richard folded his arms, and then looked straight at the window where the two women were watching. As one, they stepped back from view. When they stole another peep he was still talking with the gardener, and then he walked away, leaving the hat where it was. The gardener called over a boy who shinned up the statue and removed it.

At dinner that night Richard did not mention the hat, and not by a glance did he indicate that the incident had happened. He once again was apparently in a mood to be entertaining, and his easy conversation passed the meal pleasantly enough. Serena said little, but from time to time Janine was aware of her aunt's eyes upon her, their expression sleek and sly. Janine ignored it; there was nothing else she could do unless she asked her aunt outright if there was something on her mind—which she would not do in front of her grandfather.

Sir Adam folded his napkin. "The ball," he said suddenly. "I trust the arrangements are well in hand, Serena?"

"They are, and the invitations sent out."

"By God, I'm looking forward to it."

Serena sighed. "Are you attending as Charles the Second *again?*"

"Of course, it pleases me to be the Merry Monarch. It gives me the right to buss every pretty wench I take a fancy to—and get away with it!"

Janine smiled at that. "What shall you go as, my lady?" she asked Serena, thinking that maybe a tiny olive branch would not go amiss.

Serena's eyes slid reluctantly to her. "I haven't decided."

Sir Adam snorted. "Yes, you have! Oh, yes you have—I've been peeping. You're going as Diana, complete with bow and quiver!"

Serena's face went a dull red. "Oh. Yes."

"Don't be so difficult, Serena," he went on. "It was a perfectly polite and reasonable question. I see no reason why the answer could not have matched it!"

Uncomfortably, Janine excused herself from the table, wishing she'd not bothered with thoughts of olive branches at all. Richard stood and went to open the door for her.

"And contrary to your undoubted belief," he murmured so that only she could hear, "I shall *not* be going as Scaramouche."

She swept on without answering him or even indicating that she had heard.

The evening was dull and overcast, the low clouds still ran straight and swift through the low gray skies as she sat by the window of her room looking out. The tops of the moors were hidden in mist now, more uncertain and mysterious than at any other time since she had first come here. It was a forbidding landscape in the half-light of evening, and she felt the isolation of Calworth very keenly. She would stay for the Calworth Ball, and then—then she would go. Perhaps she could come back to visit her grandfather frequently, but she couldn't remain under his roof. Maybe the whole notion of coming here had been doomed from the outset, for only her grandfather was ever likely to have viewed her coming with any pleasure. Her relations with Serena were as bad as ever they had been, and those with Richard Stuart seemed to deteriorate with each encounter.

Cally brought her her hot milk, setting the tray on the windowsill beside her. "Oh, Miss Janine, you look very sad tonight."

"I am. I shall have to leave Calworth, and go back to London."

The maid lowered her eyes. "I shall miss you."

"Thank you, Cally, and I shall miss you too."

"Miss Janine, will you need me again tonight?"

"Something special to do?"

"It's my birthday, and we're having a little celebration in the kitchens."

"A party?" Janine looked up, thinking how pleasing a party would be in her present mood. She raised her eyebrows hopefully.

Cally smiled. "I *would* like to ask you, but it seems a bit uppity for a maid—"

"I'd like to come, Cally—if you'll all have me down

there. I won't put a damper on the fun, though, will I?"

"Oh, no, Miss Janine, you're very popular with everyone below stairs. We'd take it as a rare honor for you to come down. Only, Master Richard would frown like nobody's business—"

"That's just what it is—*nobody's* business. Except ours. And my grandfather's. I shall ask Sir Adam if I may join you, then Master Hoity-Toity can't have any objection."

Sir Adam was alone in the library, inspecting a medieval manuscript when she asked him, and he smiled, nodding. "You do as you please, my dear; your grandmother attended such occasions from time to time. It's just not done to remain for too long."

"I understand."

"Oh, by the way. After you'd gone from the dinner table, I informed Serena and Richard that I was intending accepting you once and for all as my granddaughter and therefore as my heir."

"Oh. What—?"

"Richard accepted willingly enough, but Serena is in high dudgeon. She's taking herself to see her sick sister-in-law in Kent for an indefinite period."

"Oh, dear."

"She is already having her things packed and intends leaving this very night—nothing else will suffice."

"But, it's getting late—"

"Oh, let the silly besom do as she pleases. She's more irritating over all this than an itch I can't reach. Perhaps a sojourn in Kent will bring her to her senses. Anyway, Serena's antics are her concern and shall not disturb anyone else. Go to Cally's party, my dear, and enjoy yourself." He took her hand and squeezed it suddenly. "And how is it between you and Richard now?"

"I doubt that it could possibly be worse. But I'll survive."

"That's my girl." He kissed her cheek. "Run along then."

The kitchens were warm and close after the day's cooking, and the air hung with the smell of roast beef and coffee. Janine put on her plainest dress so as not to look too much above-stairs, and she tied her hair back with a yellow ribbon to match the gown.

Her arrival at the top of the kitchen stairs caused a momentary silence, but Cally's delighted welcome soon smoothed the awkwardness over, and Janine melted into the gathering with great delight. It was light, easy company, laughing and joking, chattering and giggling, just as the theater parties had been. It was not the confined space of the theater dressing room, though, or even the stage itself. It was the warm, low-beamed kitchens of Calworth—but the atmosphere was the same. When Mrs. Bentley, the plump, rosy-cheeked cook, offered her a glass of her best elderberry wine, perhaps she would have been wiser to refuse, but everything was so congenial to Janine that she accepted with alacrity. The wine was rich and sweet, and slid smoothly down as she laughed at the acrobatics of one of the garden boys. He stood on his hands on a table, walking around with his legs jerking up and down all the time.

Cally shyly introduced her to her betrothed, the stern-faced Tom Mayhew of Edge Farm. Tom's stern expression, however, seemed to hide a warm nature, for he fussed around Cally as attentively as any gentleman would fuss around a lady. Someone produced a squeeze box and began to play, and by this time enough elderberry wine, sloe gin and various other concoctions had been consumed for quite a number of couples to begin the dancing. They paused now and then for Cally's health to be drunk, and then the dancing continued. Mrs. Bentley clapped her hands at the stroke of eleven, and a veritable feast of delicacies was carried in state from a storeroom, including a special cream cake for Cally. The dancing and merriment continued as they ate, for nothing was to be allowed to break the atmosphere of jollification. The minutes ticked by and Janine didn't give a thought to the time, and when Jethro Arkwright plucked up courage to ask her to dance, she put down her fifth glass of elderberry wine and joined him on the floor.

The tune which was playing was one she liked; and she hummed it as she danced and Jethro watched her, smiling. "I'll never forget your mother accepting my violets like that," he said suddenly. "One of the best times of my life. She sang—oh, what were it now—oh, yes. That one about being too saucy for heaven. You know the one?"

"Oh, yes. She finished her shows with it a lot."

"Do—do you know the words proper like? The way she sang them?"

"Yes. Shall I sing it?" The offer slid out quite naturally, without any thought. The feeling of warmth and relaxation filled her and she was caught up in the easy camaraderie of these people. It was so welcome and enjoyable after the stiffer, more remote behavior up in the state rooms above.

Jethro forgot his place too, and too much heady wine had been consumed by everyone there for anyone to think it was wrong. He clapped his hands and announced that Janine would sing her mother's song, and the news was greeted with claps and cheers which rang around the basements.

"A stage," said Janine. "I must have a stage."

"The table," suggested someone, and in a moment she was standing on the long, scrubbed table which had been hastily cleared of plates and glasses.

The squeeze box struck the necessary chord and began to play the tune Jethro wanted. Janine was herself again as she struck Peg's pose, her skirts held cheekily and her thick dark hair loose.

> *"I'm too wicked for them up there, I make 'em*
> *   blush and stare!*
> *With my bad, bad ways and lack of bloomin'*
> *   stays, I give 'em vapors for days and days!"*

She sauntered along the table to the accompaniment of whistles and cheers, twisting her skirts to show her shapely ankles. Everyone was laughing and clapping in time to the tune.

She rolled her eyes, leaning forward and lowering her voice just as Peg had done.

> *" 'Tis down below that I'm gonna 'ave to go,*
> *   where only sulphur winds do blow—*
> *And where it's Old Nick will be welcoming me,*
> *   with me patches, and rouge and me dimpled*
> *   knee!"*

With a flourish of yellow muslin and white underskirts, she showed one knee as the finale of the song, and as the applause broke out again, a door slammed loudly at the top of the stairs.

Silence fell over the gathering immediately as everyone looked up at Richard Stuart. Janine slowly lowered her skirts, looking at the fury on his face as he slowly descended toward them. Maids and footmen stepped away to make room for him to pass, and quite suddenly a pin could have been heard dropping in the kitchens.

He stood by the table, his hands on his hips as he looked up at Janine. "Get down."

Slowly she obeyed him, and as she stood on the floor at last, he seized her arm and propelled her toward the stairs, half pushing and half dragging her up them.

"Let me go!" she cried, tears springing to her eyes as his hard fingers dug into her flesh.

He ignored her, shoving her bodily through the door and into the hallway. Still ignoring her cries, he forced her up the staircases to the bedrooms, and at her own door he pushed her inside and came in too.

Rubbing her arm, she turned on him. "Don't you ever touch me like that again!"

"I'll touch you whenever and however it pleases me to, if I catch you behaving like a slut again!"

"A *slut?*"

"Cavorting like a harlot, showing your legs for every kitchen boy to ogle! By God, the day you took it into your empty head to descend into your grandfather's life was a bad day for all of us!"

The wine still held her in its unwary grip, and she crossed the room, striking his face with all the force she could muster. His head snapped back, and as she raised her hand again he suddenly struck her instead.

"I warned you, madam," he said softly, catching her by the shoulders and shaking her.

The ribbon fell from her hair and the shaking sent the dark curls everywhere in confusion. There were tears in her eyes as she stared up into his face without another word.

He held her for a moment and then his fingers relaxed their grip as he turned to go.

Her whisper was quite clear. "Being drunk is the only way to be happy beneath the same roof as you, Richard Stuart."

The door closed softly behind him.

Chapter 17

As she was lying in her bed the next morning, working up courage to face Richard Stuart across the breakfast table, her grandfather suddenly came to her room. Her heart dropped immediately—for she thought Richard had told him of her conduct—but he'd come on a different matter.

"Good morning, my dear, I've just come to say I'm off to Sheriff Bolton to see a friend of mine, the rector there. Name of Hawkin Sperring. His Latin's better than mine, perhaps *he* can decipher that cursed manuscript. I'll not be back until the early hours, so I probably won't see you again until breakfast tomorrow. Did Cally Arkwright's celebration go well?"

He didn't know anything about it— "Yes, very well."

He nodded. "Something else has gone very well too—Serena. Like a Spanish galleon—and just as rotund. However, no doubt her miff will not last too long, they don't usually."

"This is hardly a miff, Grandfather."

He dropped a kiss on her forehead. "It is. Good-bye then."

"Good-bye."

She lay there, looking at the sunlight streaming through the drawn curtains. Outside, the birds were singing, and the harpsichordist was practicing, the dainty notes drifting on the warm morning air. Cally came in humming cheerfully, the night's incident placed well behind her. She had come to Janine the night before, nervous and a little frightened of Richard's anger, but apart from chiding them for the noise, he'd said nothing more. It was only on Janine that his real fury had fallen.

The maid put down the fresh bowl of carnations, arranging them to their best advantage. "Tom takes over Edge Farm this morning. He's to meet Master Richard there at ten," she said, unable to contain her excitement any longer. "Tom's said we'll wed at the end of the year!" She twirled, her eyes shining.

"And there's you with your rattling about letting your eye rove over Lord Talbot!" reminded Janine, smiling. But a sudden thought seized her. Her grandfather was away for the day, and Richard for the morning. What better chance would she have of going over to see Mark at Talbot Castle? It was a good day for a ride, and the thought of the company of someone who was friendly and sympathetic was suddenly very tempting.

"After breakfast, Cally, I shall ride over to see Lord Talbot," she said.

The ride to Talbot Castle was accomplished in brilliant sunshine. She found the track beyond the Dog Stone, and followed it at a steady trot. What had Cally said? First left and second right? She rode on down the slope of the land until she suddenly saw the castle on its spur ahead.

It was a sturdy, rugged square-towered building, its battlements fiercely jutting against its roofs. Scree fell away below it, making it as secure as any moated fortress, and from its only vulnerable side the gardens of later centuries stretched. The track wound around through a marshy meadow and up through an avenue of trees to the lower drawbridge, which was more ornamental than anything else as it had no moat to bridge.

She reined in in the courtyard where grooms came to take Gemine away, and then she stood there, looking around. This was where Angela Talbot had lived—

"Janine?"

She turned to see Mark hobbling toward her on a walking-stick.

"Whatever's wrong with your leg?" she asked.

He drew her hand through his arm. "Damned great horse trod on my foot." He grinned sheepishly. "It hurts like hell too! I'm assured I'll be able to bend a toe or two by the time the day of the ball arrives, so keep a good many dances free for me, won't you?"

"Out of pity, I will," she said with a smile.

"Damn your pity," he said, leading her into the castle.

It was dark and low after the grandeur of Calworth, but its passages twisted up and down intriguingly, and there seemed no end to some of them as they wound around towers and halls.

In a fairly large chamber which had been furnished as a very comfortable drawing room, its walls hung with Flemish tapestries, he ushered her into a chair.

"Now then, what brings you to my lair?"

"I wanted to see if you would still speak to a Winterton after the other day."

"Wintertons, yes—Stuarts? Well, there I'm not so sure. He was damnably offensive. Can't think what she ever saw in him." He nodded at a portrait hanging opposite the window.

Angela Talbot was as golden-haired and green-eyed as her brother, but there was a softness and beauty in the painted face which smiled at Janine. She sat on a gilt sofa, diamond bracelets on her elegant wrists, and her lithe body revealed by the Empire lines of her mauve gown. Her shoulders were smooth and white, her neck long and graceful. She was very beautiful, very distant and very formidable. Janine stared at the painting. If Richard had loved this magnificent woman whose every fiber was one of high birth and lineage, then small wonder he had nothing but contempt for an actress' daughter—

Mark watched her and then poured two glasses of Burgundy, limping across to press one into her hand. "I wish I could help you, Janine," he said gently. "But it's not from me that you want anything, is it?"

She met his eyes. "No," she whispered.

"Damn him to hell," he murmured.

"I wish I had more sense than to feel as I do," she said with a self-conscious laugh.

"We none of us can *choose* such things, I think," he said. "Besides, he's the one without sense. Come on, enough gloom and despondency. Drink up and we'll take a walk in the sunshine. There are some roses out there which my gardeners have created over the years and which not even London hothouses can boast!"

It was good to be in his company, walking arm-in-arm around the lovely gardens. From the other side of the castle's spur of land she could see a village, Talbot Magna, which over the centuries had grown up around the fortress. Small fields had been tended in the wide valley, outlined by rough stone walls, and the gray roofs clustered together as if preparing for the worst bitterness of a Yorkshire winter.

They sat for a while in a summer house, and they hardly noticed that the sun had become hazy and there were misty clouds forming all over the skies. Mark looked up first, looking all along a far escarpment where the clouds were gathering menacingly.

"I don't like the look of the weather," he said suddenly. "I think you'd best begin your ride back to Calworth. I can't ride with you, but I'll have a groom——"

"No, it won't take me long to get back, and I'd rather be alone, truly I would."

Gemine kept a steady pace up the moor from Talbot, and Janine looked above at the skies. The clouds were silent and there was no breath of wind, just a clammy warmth which was unpleasant. Not a blade of grass stirred, and the gorse was so still it could have been made of wax. There did not even seem to be any birds, not a curlew, to break the awful quiet. She took the first left turning and urged Gemine into a canter. The horizon seemed indistinct—rain maybe— As she rode it suddenly struck her that she'd taken the wrong turning, that she recognized nothing around her and there was no sign of the Dog Stone anywhere. She turned, retracing her steps, the beginnings of fear beginning to rise within her as she saw that the horizon was closing in all around in a stealthy white mist.

Gemine cantered past the first turning, but when she reached the next fork her mind was a blank. What had Cally said? First right and second left? No, first left and second right! So, this way around it could be first right—and, second— She looked around. First left and second right again. She urged Gemine on along the track, watching anxiously for sight of the Dog Stone, the only definite landmark she would recognize.

The mist was thickening, turning the colors to muted tones which faded into white nothingness at about fifty yards. It touched her face with cold, damp fingers as it curled closer, deadening the air still more until everything was silent as a tomb. She reined in as she saw the Dog Stone at last, turning Gemine from the track toward it. If she remained by it, she'd be safe until the mist had gone—it was all she could think of.

The indistinct pillar of stone remained hazy the whole time she rode slowly toward it, and by the time she dismounted by its reassuring solidity, the mist was so thick she could hardly see her hand before her face.

She leaned against it thankfully, listening to the silence. Gemine snorted nearby and she looked for the horse, but in that moment the mare had wandered out of sight in the gloom.

"Gemine? Gemine?"

She could hear the horse, but that was all, and she did not dare to leave the safety of the stone. The minutes passed and she couldn't even hear the horse anymore.

Something small rustled in the undergrowth, the mist magnifying that tiny rustling until it sounded frightening. Biting her lip, she pressed miserably against the standing stone, wishing she'd accepted Mark's offer of a groom to ride with her. How long would the mist last? It swirled eagerly around her, like an ethereal vine, writhing slowly and coiling endlessly.

The quiet was broken terrifyingly by the scrambling rattle of the scree and the frightened whinnying of the horse. The slithering terror went on for what seemed like a minute or more as Janine listened in horror, but then it was silent again. "Gemine?" she screamed suddenly, her voice coming back at her from echoing rocks unseen beyond her small space. "Gemine?"

Nothing. The thick silence settled over the moor again.

Janine slid to the ground, huddling her arms around her knees, and burying her face in the folds of golden velvet. She curled up as tightly as she could to shut out the fear—fear that the mist would last for days and she'd be alone by the Dog Stone—

How long she huddled there she did not know, for the passage of time seemed so slow and labored, with neither light nor dark, nor any shadow to tell how far the day had progressed.

"Janine?"

The voice was distant, and she raised her head swiftly. From which direction had it come?

"Janine?"

It was Richard, she was sure it was. "Richard? *Richard!*"

"Don't move, whatever you do, don't move!"

Her hands moved over the damp, cold surface of the stone. "I'm by the Dog Stone!" she cried, still uncertain of which direction his voice had come. She was on the edge of crying, her heart thundering with relief. A faint light glimmered through the mist, a red flame.

"Janine? Call again!"

"Over here, Richard, I'm over here!"

The torch moved steadily closer and then she could see the horsemen. They loomed from the mist like ghosts, but the gentle sound of their horses on the turf was welcomingly solid. The torches smoked strangely in the mist and it seemed to recoil from the warmth of the flames, leaping back almost to make everything clearer.

Tears were pouring down her cheeks as Richard dismounted. He took a long breath as he looked at her. "God above, woman," he said wearily, "I'll have to chain you to a stake at Calworth—you're not to be trusted an inch outside the house!"

Her shoulders shook. "Don't," she cried miserably, "oh, don't shout at me this time too, please don't! Gemine—I don't know where she is, I think she's fallen over a cliff and she's dead!"

He took her arm and pulled her close suddenly. "Don't upset yourself," he said gently. "I'm not shouting."

"Gemine—"

He looked at the cloak of mist. "We'll not see anything in this light. What did you hear?"

She sniffed, wiping her eyes with a handkerchief. "A scrambling noise, and Gemine screaming—I've never heard a horse scream before. Then everything was quiet again and I haven't heard her since." She shivered as she remembered, and he took off his coat and put it around her shoulders.

"You've had a shock," he said. "We'd better get you back to the house."

"But Gemine may be injured somewhere—"

One of the men urged his horse nearer. "I was thinking it sounds like Overton Scree, Mr. Stuart."

"Aye," he agreed softly, "so was I."

"What's Overton Scree?" she asked.

"A hundred or so yards north of here, behind large boulders, there's a sharp scree. If Gemine went over it, she'll not have survived the fall. God above, woman, staying safely by this damned stone is the only sensible thing you've done in days!"

She looked away to hide the fresh tears which were forcing their way down her cheeks again. Gemine was dead, and she'd have been safe in the stables at Calworth now if her rider had not been so foolish—

He picked her up suddenly and put her on his horse, mounting behind her.

The torches smoked and flared as the horses picked their way back to the track, moving slowly as the wavering light picked up the ruts which led safely back to Calworth.

A hot mustard bath awaited her, and a drink of warm milk which was laced with something she could not have put a name to. Whatever it was, it made her drowsy, and she made no fuss when Cally put her to bed for the rest of the day. The bed was a cocoon in which to hide away. Just for a while—

When she awoke there was bright moonlight streaming into the room, and as she looked out she saw that the moors stretched clearly for miles into the distance, bathed silver by the brightness of the moon. Above, the stars were glittering in a clear sky, and it was as if the mist had never been. She stood by the window, brushing her hair slowly as she looked out. Everything was so beautiful and peaceful, it was hard to believe the terror of earlier—

"How are you?" said Richard from the chair by the fireplace, and she turned with a start.

"I didn't know you were there!"

"I don't normally enter ladies' boudoirs uninvited, but I wanted to see you before you saw Sir Adam." He got up, leaning against the bedpost, watching her. "The mist lifted earlier and I sent some men out to look for Gemine."

The brush stopped.

"She was at the foot of Overton Scree, and they buried her there."

Tears sprang to her eyes and she turned to look blindly at the moors again.

"I wanted to see you because I'm going to tell Sir Adam that the horse broke a leg and we had to destroy her. I'd rather he didn't discover about today, about how close to death you came out there. Coming so swiftly after his shock the other day concerning you—"

"Very well," she said in a voice which shook a little.

"You've come to mean a great deal to him."

"You make that sound as if such a thing is nothing short of a miracle," she said, recovering a little.

He smiled faintly, searching in his pocket for a cigar. "Do you mind if I smoke?"

"No. Please do."

The sweet smoke spread through the room for a moment before he spoke again. "When he informed Serena and myself yesterday that he intends recognizing you formally as his heir, he made it clear that he wants me to remain here to run the estates. I love Calworth, everything about it from the meanest stony acre to the richest pasture land. I've enjoyed managing it not only because of my affection for the place but also because of my affection for the man who is master of it."

She turned to look at him. "I fail to see—"

"Where this is leading? To this. I have no wish to leave Calworth, and so maybe we should declare a truce of some sort."

She began to brush her hair again. She was so aware of him as he leaned so casually there, aware of the soft accent in his voice and the foolish desire she suddenly had to blurt out the truth of her feelings. Oh, that *would* be foolish— "There's no need for a truce," she said shortly, "for I intend leaving Calworth after the ball."

"Leaving? Why?"

"I did not come here to get my claws into an inheritance, Mr. Stuart. I came for reasons of which you are fully aware now. My stay here has been made happy only because of my grandfather, not for any other reason."

"If you're referring to Serena—"

"Yes, I am. And you—your conduct has left a great deal to be desired."

"And because of that you're prepared to leave your grandfather, after coming here and making yourself indispensable to his happiness? I salute you!" He bowed mockingly.

"You have a way of deliberately misinterpreting my every word and action, don't you? It must have taken you years of practice to become as obnoxious as you now are, unless *all* Scotsmen are born like it!"

"Some say we are. Look, you just can't leave him now, you'd break his heart. He has visions of you living here, marrying here, bringing his first great-grandchild into the world here—"

"Don't."

"Well? You *must* know that's how his mind's working! No doubt he goes further and has you wed to Mark Talbot, thus uniting the two families after all these centuries."

"I don't intend marrying Mark, I don't intend marrying *anyone!* And I don't intend remaining here, because I'm certain in my heart that everyone—including my grandfather—would live a happier life if I took myself away again and maybe only paid Calworth visits once or twice a year. My aunt despises me and has even gone to live elsewhere for the time being—"

"Serena is in a temper, that's all. She'll come round."

"Will she? I doubt it. And then there's you—you've made it quite clear that you do not particularly like me—and I think I underestimate when I say that, and that my presence is something of an irritation."

"I've not said that."

"You did not *have* to *say* it! I may be a mere woman, sir, but I'm not stupid!"

"You are if you believe I resent your presence. You have a right to be here—I've never denied that."

"Then what has your conduct been about?" she demanded.

"You have a right to be here, but you should be *worthy* of this house!"

"Apparently, in your eyes, I'm not."

He said nothing, stubbing out the cigar and loosening his cravat. "You," he said slowly, "are the second most stubborn, mule-headed woman I've ever met. First place still goes to Angela Talbot, but by God you run her a close second!" He returned to his chair and sat down, leaning his head wearily back.

"You, sir, hold first place by a distance in the Arrogance Stakes!"

He smiled without looking around at her. "Maybe I do. Angela had the gall to tell me something of that sort too."

"I begin to like her."

"No doubt. But *she* would have made your life a misery if she'd been here, she was no softy like her brother. Beautiful she may have been, and high-born, etcetera, etcetera, but she wanted to be lord and master."

"I'll warrant *that* pleased you."

"The first and only time she ever attempted to overrule one of my orders was here at Calworth. She never did it again. The engagement was terminated by mutual consent."

"Terminated? But, I thought—"

"Oh, everyone *thinks*, but they're wrong. It was finished the day before she left for London, and it soon became apparent that she'd not told anyone about it, and so I said nothing, intending to announce it on her return. The rest you know. When she died of the pox, it hardly seemed the thing to say it. So it never came out, and as far as everyone is concerned, had she lived we would have been married by now."

She came closer, standing to look down at him. "If she was like that, what on earth possessed you to propose to her in the first place? Or even *court* her in the first place?"

"You have a nosy nature, Janine Winterton."

"You are the one who began telling me about it."

"Very well. Put it down to my heart foolishly ruling my head for once. She was very beautiful, and I'm never immune to beauty." He sat forward suddenly. "Do you still intend leaving?"

"Yes. I think I must, for everyone's sake."

"Hardly for mine. Or your grandfather's. For differing reasons, of course."

"Oh, of course."

"Serena *will* come round, you know. In her heart she knows you are who you claim to be, she's just refusing to give in without a fight."

"You hardly seem to need someone to fight for you, Mr. Stuart."

"Janine, if there's to be a truce, then perhaps you should call me by my Christian name—as you did earlier today."

"Put it down to the heat of the moment," she said sarcastically.

"Sarcasm? The lowest form of wit? You disappoint me, I thought maybe talking with you would make a difference. Obviously not."

"Your notion of talking to me always ends up by talking down to what you consider to be my level, Richard."

"What are you so damned prickly for? Did you quarrel with Talbot or something?"

She sighed exasperatedly—she was annoyed with herself, and with him. With him because he was making it clear that he intended tolerating her—no more—and he seemed to think she would find that perfectly satisfactory and that she shouldn't expect any more. She was annoyed with herself for still loving him— "I'm *not* being prickly and I *haven't* quarreled with Mark, I don't quarrel with anyone except you! You bring out the very worst in me, Richard Stuart."

"So it seems. So, you're determined about going back?"

"Yes."

"Can you afford to?"

"I'll manage. I have the house in Lavender Street—"

"Oh, that reminds me, this letter came from there for you today." He took an envelope from his pocket and gave it to her. He got up. "Have you said anything to your grandfather about leaving?"

"No."

"Well, think very carefully before you do, because you're wrong about wanting to go. You don't want to go back to the theater, that's just defiant nonsense! You belong here, with him. Calworth's in your blood, Janine, and it won't be denied."

"You seem to know me better than I know myself."

"In this I do." He put his hand to her chin for a moment. "Stop and think for a while."

His touch was like a shock, and she moved away. "Do you think I haven't thought?" she said quietly. "I think about it constantly. Good night, Richard."

"Good night."

Chapter 18

She forgot about the letter until the next morning, when she awoke with a headache after a restless sleep filled with confusing, unhappy dreams. The envelope lay beside the bowl of carnations beside the bed, and it was the first thing she saw as she opened her eyes.

Sitting up, she opened the envelope, wondering what Carter could have written to her about. But the letter was not from the butler at Lavender Street, it was from David Wolfe, and as she unfolded it a check fell out onto the bed. It was for four thousand guineas, and it was made out to her. Amazed, she stared at it for a moment, and then slowly she read the accompanying letter.

Janine. My sins in your eyes must surely be multitude if you deny me even the chance to visit the house which was my second home for so long. However, I no doubt deserve your contempt. But those multitudinous sins number amongst them an inability to accept that I am unwelcome, and a hopeless regret which I pray you will one day come to believe I feel for all that I was guilty

*of. Being without Peg has been a sorry experience,
an experience which has nurtured feelings of guilty
conscience. Making amends completely is impossible, but I am attempting to do so. Lady Luck
smiled upon me at last with a royal flush at the
very moment I was about to concede defeat yet
again, and so I can return to the daughter at least
part of what I took from the mother. It's not
sufficient, by any means, but in view of my present
uncertain circumstances, I feel that unless I send
it to you now I may never be able to. Accept it in
the spirit in which it is given, my dearest Janine,
and find it in your heart to forgive me, miserable
creature that I am. I love you still, and what greater
punishment could have been meted out to me?
David.*

She read it again and then folded it and put it back
in its envelope. She didn't know what to think or what
to do. How would it look if she accepted four thousand
guineas from a man like David Wolfe? But the words
he had chosen made her feel he meant everything he
said. Maybe his conscience was too heavy to bear. But
what did he mean by his "present uncertain circumstances"? Or by saying that unless he did something
now he might never be able to?

When she went down to her breakfast she was still
undecided about the letter and the check. But about
one thing she was absolutely sure, she was not going to
say anything about it.

Her grandfather was in disgruntled mood as he sat
at the table with his beefsteak and egg. He was im-
mersed in *The Times* and seemed hardly to notice
when she came in.

"Good morning, Grandfather. Richard."

Sir Adam looked up, peering over his spectacles. "So
it's *Richard* now. Maybe I should go away more often

if improvements of that nature occur in my absence."

She helped herself to some bacon and sat down. "Did you get your manuscript sorted out?"

"No. Damned fellow couldn't do any better than me. I'll get to the bottom of it in the end, but it's damned annoying being foiled by one blasted sentence."

Richard stirred his coffee. "What is the offending document about, Sir Adam?"

"Fishing rights in a mill pond somewhere in Rutland."

Richard raised an eyebrow. "How absorbing."

The old man smiled then. "You may scoff, my boy, but I find it interesting. Very interesting. Now then, which column was I on in this fool paper. Ah, yes." He adjusted his spectacles and read again, applying himself to the beefsteak with some zest.

Richard glanced at Janine. "I read somewhere recently that a theater in London attempted to put on one of your mother's shows."

"Oh?"

"Yes, a dismal failure. A very uncertain life, the theater."

She eyed him for a moment. "Yes, it is."

"One wonders what will happen to the players performing in such a failure."

"Does one?"

"Yes. What *do* they do, Janine?"

She pressed her lips together crossly. "They manage, Richard, they manage."

"I shudder to think of a life merely *managing*, don't you?"

"Good God!" exclaimed Sir Adam suddenly. "That fellow what's-his-name, the cousin of young Talbot! You know, the one who came to dine here a year or so ago, the unsavory fellow I didn't take to but who Serena dripped over all evening!"

"Lord Wolfe?" said Richard.

Janine dropped her spoon with a clatter, and Richard glanced curiously at her.

"Yes, that's the fellow," went on Sir Adam. "Well, he's dead! Shot in a duel last week in Epping Forest of all places!"

Janine stared at the newspaper across the table. So that was David Wolfe's "uncertain circumstances," that was why he thought he would never be able to do anything unless he did it then—

"Damned fool things duels," said Sir Adam, sniffing. "Don't prove a jot about the rights and wrongs of an argument, just which idiot's the better shot. This argument was apparently about the ownership of a thoroughbred stallion, and now the other fellow and the stallion have fled the realm, and Wolfe's six foot under for his pains. Damned fools. Nothing better to do with their time. Army service would sort them out."

Janine couldn't tear her eyes away from the paper. When she'd read his letter he was already dead—

Sir Adam looked up suddenly. "Is something wrong, my dear? Did you know Wolfe?"

"Yes. I—I had a letter from him." She had not intended to say it, but the shock of what she'd just heard made her unwary.

Richard leaned back, looking closely at her suddenly. "A friend of yours, was he?"

"I—In a manner of speaking."

"In what manner precisely?"

"He was more my mother's friend than mine."

Sir Adam grunted. "Well, the world knows Peg Oldfield was a law unto herself. The fellow was a cad, to my mind, and I trust *you* were not on close terms with him, Janine."

"No, I wasn't."

"Just as well. I can't say I'd have approved of that, not in the slightest."

Richard said nothing more, but he continued to look

at her from time to time as if he suspected there was far more to the story than she was admitting.

Sir Adam went on with his paper for a while and then put away his spectacles. "That's an end to my sitting for this meal, I fancy. God above, you know, I never thought I'd say it, but I actually miss that silly old besom of a sister! Her rattle was a comforting background noise at times. When's she coming back, I wonder?"

"Her dudgeons are very high, Sir Adam," said Richard.

"I know, dear boy, I *know*," said the old man with some feeling.

The newspaper tucked under his arm, he left the breakfast room, but in a moment he was back again. "Richard? I must speak privately with you sometime today."

"Yes, Sir Adam? At what time?"

"Any time, my boy, any time. I shall be in the library all day."

Janine went for a walk after breakfast. It was a blustery day, the wind snatching at her skirts as she walked on the lower slopes of the moors, stopping to sit on a rock to look across the valley at Calworth. The deer roamed in the park and the trees bent and swayed as the wind pounced on their boughs. The smell of the moors was fresh and pungent, a mixture of flowers and damp earth, and high above the curlews cried excitedly as they rode the currents. Calworth stretched across its hillside, bright in the sunlight, its copper dome half green, half red-gold. Was Richard right about her feelings for this place? *Was* it in her blood now? Were her yearnings for the life of the theater something she was clinging to because she was unhappy? Maybe she should give herself more time here—after all, if and when she returned to the theater, she would have enough money to manage on now. She bent to pick a sprig of pink heather, twisting it between her fingers until the colors were a spinning blur. She would accept David Wolfe's letter, and the check, for now there was no denying the spirit in which it was given. Maybe she *should* forgive him. Peg had.

She walked back to the house, still deep in thought. But when she opened the door of her room to go in, she was brought abruptly and angrily back to the present.

Richard stood by her bed, David's letter in his hand, and he had obviously been reading it.

"Is it your practice to read other people's letters?" she asked furiously, snatching it from him.

"Not usually," he said, "but this is one occasion upon which I thought I would break that rule. And how glad I am that I did! So, he wasn't a close friend? How does it come then that he speaks of still loving you? A man doesn't love without managing to get close, Miss Winterton!"

"You are insulting, sirrah!"

"How close did he get?" he said, seizing her arm and making her look at him.

"Let go!"

"How close!" His fingers dug in more firmly.

"As close as I am to you now," she hissed, "so that the contempt and disbelief I see in your eyes right now, *he* could see in mine! If you don't let go I shall scream that you are attacking me, and believe me, I'm actress enough to give a virtuoso performance!"

He released her, almost thrusting her away. "Oh, I believe that last statement, Miss Winterton. After all, is that not what you have been giving ever since you came here? A virtuoso performance indeed!"

"Get out of this room," she whispered. "Just get out and leave me alone."

"It *would* be a pleasure, madam, but I intend getting to the bottom of this business."

"Well *I* do not intend telling you. Unless you are about to beat me to have your way, you had best go."

"You'll never be worthy of this house, Miss Winterton!" he breathed.

"Beat it out of me, or go!" she repeated, staring past him, her face wooden. But inside she felt as if her heart were breaking.

As he reached the door, he paused. "*Was* there anything between you and Wolfe?"

"Would you believe me if I said no? The truce did not last long, did it, Richard? And you are the one who apparently believes we may all live amicably side by side. The days of miracles are gone."

She heard the door close, and she stood in the center of the room fighting back the tears.

Chapter 19

"Ah, Richard, there you are at last, I'd begun to think you'd forgotten," said Sir Adam, carefully putting away his manuscript. "A glass of cognac?"

Richard nodded.

"I've a proposition to put to you, and I don't want you to say anything until I've finished. Now then, shall we sit down by the fire? I know, a fire in the middle of summer, but this damned library's cold today and my old joints need warming."

They sat by the fire, and Sir Adam swirled his cognac for a moment. "I don't know quite how to put this to you, but I must, for it means so much to me. I'm master of Calworth, I live for this house, just as I believe you do. I may be wrong."

"I feel about the house as you do, Sir Adam."

Sir Adam nodded. "Then you will understand that I am an old man now, indeed there are very few of the friends of my youth still alive. What happens to Calworth when I am gone is a matter which keeps me awake in my bed at nights. Awake and concerned."

"There should be no concern, Sir Adam. The house

will go to your granddaughter and then, I suspect, to Lord Talbot."

"No. No, I don't want a Talbot lording it here. It goes against the grain—I was almost damned glad when that insufferable Angela snuffed it of the pox. Forgive me, my boy, but she was an impossible choice for you and I think you may consider yourself lucky to have escaped perdition."

Richard smiled faintly. "I have already acknowledged the debt I owe to luck, Sir Adam."

"So, there are to be no Talbot hounds in Calworth kennels, Richard. I like Mark, but I do not want him marrying Janine. That the notion to have her is in his mind is all too plain; you can see that when he looks at her. He's smitten—with a vengeance."

"I know. But if they wish to marry—"

"Janine don't want Talbot!"

Richard offered him a cigar and lit one for himself, sitting back with the cognac. "That's not how it appears to me. However—"

"It's immaterial, Richard, because I want *you* to marry her. No, hear me out. Janine is very dear to me, as dear as the house itself. She must remain here because she's a Winterton, the only Winterton after me. I know my great-grandchildren will not be Wintertons, but there is nothing on God's earth I'd prefer more than for them to be Stuarts. Marry her, Richard, and then Calworth will be yours, as I had always intended it should be."

Richard lowered his glass in amazement. "I don't believe I'm hearing correctly, Sir Adam—"

"Yes, you are. If you want Calworth, you'll marry my granddaughter. Unless you do, you'll have nothing."

"An ultimatum?"

"I suppose it is. An old man don't have too much time to manipulate, to wait around in the hope that something will come up. I'm not a gambling man, my boy, but I'm ruthless and ambitious enough when it suits me. I want you and Janine here, and if it requires pressure from me to achieve that, then I will use pressure."

"My answer is no, Sir Adam. I will not be forced into a marriage I don't want. I will marry the bride *I* choose, not the one someone else chooses for me. Janine may be very beautiful, and an heiress to attract half the titled names in the realm, but *I* don't want her. If this means refusing your ultimatum, then that is understood on both sides. I will remain at Calworth during your lifetime, Sir Adam; I will look after the running of the estates as well and as diligently as I have done until now. But after that, I will leave."

Sir Adam pursed his lips. "If it's because of this business with Wolfe—?"

"You know about that?"

"She told me. You wrong her, Richard."

"I still do not want her as my wife, Sir Adam."

"Forget the ultimatum," said Sir Adam wearily. "It was a vain hope that you'd be intimidated. But you're a fool, turning down an offer like that, an offer which would make you a very rich man."

Richard glanced up at the balcony suddenly and saw Janine standing there. She turned and walked away and Sir Adam knew nothing of her having been there. The old man swirled his cognac and sniffed it. "I suppose I shall have to resign myself to great-grandchildren by the name of Talbot then. God curse it!"

Richard caught up with her in the gardens. "Janine?" She turned. "Yes?"

Her eyes were bright, and she looked away quickly lest he see how close she was to tears.

"How long were you there?"

"Long enough."

"I'm sorry you heard—"

"I'm not. For it gives *me* the chance to say to you, sir, that nothing on God's earth would make me marry you, so your refusal would have been matched by mine. I find you odious in the extreme, and sharing a bed with you would be like sharing a nest with a snake!"

He took a long breath. "Well, we would seem to be in agreement, then."

"We most certainly are. I trust you did not imagine I was party to my grandfather's plan."

"It hadn't occurred to me one way or the other."

"Very little of any importance ever seems to occur to you, Richard Stuart. You are most probably oatcake between the ears."

"If you protest much more, Miss Winterton, I shall begin to think you are miffed that I've refused a match with you."

"You'd be flattering yourself, then," she retorted, her chin up defiantly. If ever she had needed brilliance at acting, it was now—

Unexpectedly, he smiled. "Maybe I would at that," he said. "One thing I must admit, though, and that is that I have yet to find my encounters with you dull!"

"I'm an actress, I'm trained to keep my audience enthralled," she said acidly, walking away from him, "no matter how dull-witted that audience may be."

At luncheon she kept up her act, bubbling with conversation just as she had once seen Peg do after a bitter argument with David Wolfe. No one, especially not Richard Stuart, was going to guess how broken-hearted and rejected she really felt. If he sensed anything artificial about her apparent carefree mood, he gave not the slightest indication, taking little interest in her. It was not until Mark Talbot drove over in his curricle to ask

Janine out for a drive with him that Richard showed any concern in her activities.

Mark climbed awkwardly down from the curricle, smiling at Janine as she came to greet him.

"I thought maybe a visit to Leyworth Goat Fair would prove a good excuse to call upon you," he said, raising her hand to his lips.

"A *goat* fair?"

"Originally that's all it was, but now there are many more interesting things than mere goats to entertain you. Shall you come?"

She smiled and nodded, turning as Richard and her grandfather came down the steps to the curricle. "I'm invited to Leyworth Goat Fair," she said to Sir Adam.

"Heavens, is it that time of the year again? Dash me, I suppose it must be. Well, I'm too old for such fool things. Shall you go, Richard?"

Richard glanced frostily at Mark and then shook his head slightly. "Maybe later, there's a good filly for sale in Leyworth." He bowed. "I've work to attend to. Talbot. Janine."

He went back up the steps, and Sir Adam cleared his throat. "Yes, well, I don't know what the ice is for between you and Richard, Mark, but I trust it ain't nothing serious."

Mark smiled faintly. "I don't know what's the matter with him, Sir Adam, but I can be as stubbornly obstinate as any Scot and shall continue as long as he does. Talbots may bow occasionally to Wintertons, but certainly not to Stuarts."

Janine felt uncomfortable, for she knew the awkwardness dated from the day she and Mark had ridden to the Dog Stone. "I—I'll go and get ready, Mark."

Inside she came face to face with Richard on the stairs, and the look in his eyes as he stepped aside for her to pass was too obvious for her to ignore. "Well?"

she said provocatively. "Are you going to *say* it, or merely *look* it?"

"What?" he asked, folding his arms and leaning against the wrought-iron gold banisters.

"That I'm behaving forwardly by going out alone with Mark, and that once again I'm merely confirming your low opinion of me."

His eyes flickered. "You said it, Janine, not I," he murmured, going on down the stairs and leaving her standing there furiously trying to think of a suitable retort.

A short while later she came down in a green-and-white-checkered silk gown and light shawl. Cally had dressed her hair in two bunches of ringlets on either side of her head, and the ribbons of her bonnet came behind them, making them bounce as she descended the steps to where Mark and Sir Adam still stood talking by the curricle. She pulled on her white gloves as she reached them.

"I hope I didn't take too long?" she said.

Mark's eyes moved appreciatively over her. "If you did, Janine, it was well worth the wait."

The curricle skimmed along the track behind the two black, high-stepping horses whose trotting exceeded the canter of lesser horses. She retied her bonnet as the wind tugged at its frothy flowers and brim. The meadow grass grew high on either side of the narrow lane, and cow parsley like sweet-smelling white lace. With the swift, breathless moments of the journey her mood began to lighten, and for a while she could forget Richard Stuart.

Leyworth was a market town on the banks of a river. It stretched up a single cobbled street to a marketplace with an ancient cross in the center of it. Beyond it was the stout tower of the church at the top of the hill. The fair was in the square, a huddle of canvas-topped stalls, tents, noise, smells and color. Goats and sheep bleated in pens, dogs barked as the stage-coach set off noisily for York, people laughed and tradesmen shouted their wares. The smell of hot pies, gingerbread, toffee apples, leather goods, spilled ale and fried onions mingled with less pleasant odors in a jumble of interest which was almost bewildering as the nervous team came to a standstill outside the Three Angels tavern. An ostler led them to the yard behind, catching the coin Mark flicked to him.

Mark leaned on his walking stick. "Damned foot," he grumbled. "It's nearly healed, but if I don't use a stick it gives me a bad time."

"Let's just walk around for a while then, and then I'll be quite happy just to sit and watch."

"You seem to be proving an economic prospect," he said with a smile. "I'm almost tempted to propose, for with a wife like you with the pursestrings, my fortune would be forever safe."

She smiled at him. "Don't tempt your luck, in my present mood I just might accept."

They walked between the cluttered stalls, watching the wheel of fortune, the dice games, the cock fight behind one of the tents and the stall selling paper windmills which had a crowd of small children, all staring open-mouthed at the pretty colors whirling on their stick pins.

As they sat beneath a tree afterward, watching some traveling acrobats, Janine spoke of David Wolfe.

"I'm sorry he died, Mark."

"You know about it then?"

"My grandfather read it in *The Times*."

"David had tried his luck in a duel before, he nearly lost his life then. He should have learned the lesson I did, but obviously not. Dueling is a gentleman's sport and more often than not a gentleman's death. I survived. Twice. He did not. The desire to pick quarrels must be in the blood, eh?"

"He wrote to me before the duel," she said, not liking to pursue the point, although she was curious to learn that Mark had been prepared to duel.

"Oh?" He glanced at her, his hair a bright gold in the dappled sunlight flashing through the leaves above them.

She lowered her eyes. "He was a friend of my mother's, you know that."

"I know. News travels, especially within a family."

"He sent me a check for four thousand guineas."

"Did he, be damned? Why?"

"Oh, he—borrowed from my mother once. He was returning it. He was already dead by the time I received the letter."

"And that upsets you now?"

"In a way. It—it was a nice letter. I almost felt guilty for having thought badly of him."

"No doubt that was the idea," he said with a sly grin. "David knew how to play upon women's feelings. By God he did. If I'd that talent I'd be employing it on you myself."

"Oh, you've a talent, Mark Talbot. Ive been watching the women here today, and you are like a magnet. Heads turn as if swiveled when you pass by with your big green eyes and golden hair. They'd all be clay in your hands if you wanted."

"But not you?"

"Well, I'm just a nincompoop without any sense," she said with a smile.

"You must be—to fall for a fellow like Stuart. Can't understand it, when I'm here, ready and waiting—and by God, more than willing." He tweaked her cheek laughingly, but she knew he wanted far more than a playful banter to pass between them.

They drove home as the shadows were just beginning to lengthen. The lacework patterns of the trees and hedgerows lay warmly across the dusty lane as the team trotted spankingly after their rest.

As they turned a corner, she saw the pool. It was limpid beneath its fringe of low-hanging trees, with hardly a ripple to mar its mirror surface.

"Oh, look," she cried, touching his arm. "I didn't see that going the other way!"

He reined in. "You wouldn't, those elderberry bushes are in the way. Do you want to stop for a while?"

"Yes, it's so lovely."

"There's a legend, you know," he said, as he tooled the stamping team from the lane and into the field where the buttercups and grasses grew waist high.

"I can tell by your tone that I shall not like the legend."

"Well, it will make you look twice at that mysterious, dark water," he murmured, rolling his eyes.

"Go on with you, there's no legend," she said firmly.

"Oh, but there is." He handed her down from the blue curricle, and they walked through the thick, lush meadow toward the tree-fringed pool. "It's said that one day, centuries ago, a parson was traveling home and he stopped to rest awhile by Dragongarth Pool. He had his poor meal beside the waters, and lay back to rest awhile. It was a balmy evening, just as this is now. It was peaceful and beautiful. As it is now."

"Yes?" she said suspiciously, suspecting a leg-pull at the end.

"He lay back, no doubt contemplating his next pulpit-thundering sermon, and the wind died away—as it has right now. Not a leaf stirred, not a blade of grass moved in the silence. The birds were cowed by something—he knew not what."

She stared at him, held by the hypnotic quality of his voice. "What happened?"

"He heard nothing, sensed nothing. Until—a sense

of foreboding crept over him. He sat up. Very, very slowly. And he saw a beautiful maiden, sitting on a rock in the middle of the pool. She was singing, but he only sensed that she was, and she was combing her hair with a golden comb. She was the most perfect creature the parson had ever seen, and he called to her, wanting to know her name."

He paused and she waited. "Well? What happened?"

"She turned towards him, and he felt an uncontrollable desire to be out there with her, and so he began to wade into the dark, cold waters. Deeper and deeper. But he could not help himself, he *had* to be there with the maiden. But as he struggled, the water began to suck him down into its fathomless depths, and he reached out a desperate hand to her— The last thing he saw before the water closed over him was that she was not a maiden, but a foul—and fearsome—water DRAGON!"

He shouted the last word and she jumped as if someone had put ice down her back. "You beast! There's no such tale!" she cried, half laughing, half nervous.

"Oh, yes, there is. Hush. Look." He lowered his voice again and pointed at the pool.

Her eyes were huge as she looked. It *was* quiet here, and the trees hardly moved. There weren't even any birds singing— She turned, gathering her green and white skirts to hurry back toward the curricle, but he caught her, laughing, and they tumbled into the long grass.

He leaned over her. "There *is* such a tale," he murmured. "But it must have been the parson's horse who told it."

"Mark Talbot, I should poke you on your nose for that!" She laughed.

"Am I good enough for the stage then?"

"On that performance, yes. Too good!"

He said nothing, looking down at her as she lay there, her bonnet awry and her hairpins undone. "I love you, Janine Winterton, but then I think you know that already, don't you?"

"Mark—"

He smiled. "I'm Talbot to the core, I *will* not see defeat staring me in the face. Now, maybe I'd best spirit you back to Calworth before Stuart has the hounds out again." He bent his head to kiss her gently on the cheek.

"Get up!" snapped a voice, and a shadow fell across them.

"Stuart!" Mark got up, helping Janine to her feet.

She knew that she presented a sorry sight, but she stood there meeting his scornful gaze, her head up and her eyes steady.

He pointed at a black phaeton waiting in the lane. "Get in, Janine."

She didn't move, and Mark stepped forward. "By God, Stuart, this is the final straw!"

"I doubt, my dear Talbot, whether you are in a position to argue with me. You have gravely overstepped the bounds of good behavior here in this meadow today, and I intend putting an end to these goings-on."

"Goings-on?" she breathed furiously.

His hazel eyes swung from Mark to her. "Yes, madam. I find you cavorting in the grass, in a manner to cause serious doubts as to what may have happened had I *not* come along when I did! One look at yourself should tell you exactly what I mean."

Mark suddenly clenched his fist and struck out, catching Richard squarely on the jaw.

"Mark!" she cried in horror.

But he struck again, not giving Richard time to recover. The suddenness of the attack caught Richard unaware, but he was not slow to fight back. The two swung at each other again and Janine ran to force herself between them, pushing them apart.

"Stop it! Stop it!" she cried, almost in tears. "*Please!*"

Mark lowered his fists. "Take back what you hinted at then, Stuart!" he said in a low voice which revealed the real depths of his anger.

"I take nothing back, Talbot."

"Then you shall hear from my seconds."

"No, Mark, please, no." She seized his hands. "Don't say that! It's not worth it. Please, Richard."

Richard rubbed his jaw where Mark had hit him. "If he wishes to call me out, madam, it is his privilege to do so."

She looked from one angry face to the other in desperation. "No," she said, "no. I'll not allow it. Mark, don't call him out, I beg of you. For my sake don't call him out."

Richard looked exasperatedly at her. "For heaven's sake, woman, stop interfering! Step back and let this be settled!"

"I'll interfere for as long as it takes to make you both see some sense. You heard what my grandfather said about dueling—it proves nothing about the rights and wrongs of the argument, merely which man is the better marksman. And you, Mark, said today that you would have thought David had learned his lesson about the futility of dueling. Both of you know better."

Mark squeezed her shaking fingers. "I'm convinced, sweetheart," he said quietly. "Now go and get into his phaeton. I think it's best if you go back to Calworth with him."

"But—"

"No arguments."

She looked up into his face for a moment and then turned to go to the phaeton with its team of dapples.

Richard looked at Mark. "Stay away from her, Mark."

"Why? Is she your property?"

"No. She's Calworth's heir, and her name must have no unsavory rumor attached to it."

"Calworth's guardian now, are you? Well, I'll tell you this once and once only, Richard. I love her, and as long as she accepts my company I will see her. My intentions are not dishonorable in the slightest. Sir Adam makes no complaint about me calling upon her, so I fail to see why you take it upon yourself to do anything, especially as your personal interest in Janine seems to be nonexistent beyond making her life a misery. There will be no blood shed this time maybe, but I swear, Richard, that if anything of this kind happens again, then no amount of pleading on her part will make me step down from a confrontation."

"I do not doubt that—a man who has emerged the victor from two duels with good marksmen must surely be proven brave."

Mark smiled faintly. "I'm a good marksman right enough, but I learned that duels merely satisfy temper and nothing else—which is why I find it hard to step down from you right now. Next week I shall come to the Calworth Ball, and I shall behave as if none of this has happened. I trust that you will do the same."

"I shall. But do not ever compromise her again, Mark."

Richard inclined his head and walked slowly through the long grass toward the phaeton where Janine sat stiffly, staring at the horses' ears.

Neither of them said a word during the remainder of the journey back to Calworth, and as the phaeton swayed to a standstill outside the house, she climbed down without waiting for him to help her. She ran up the steps and inside without a backward glance.

Chapter 20

She said nothing to Cally of what had happened. And when she dressed for dinner that evening, she felt more like pleading a headache and avoiding facing Richard again that day than she had ever done before. But such a show of funk would probably be regarded by him as an acknowledgment of his triumph, and so she chose her gown and behaved as if everything were perfectly all right.

When the footman duly presented himself at her door to escort her to the state room for *apéritifs* she was ready. The gown she had chosen was a soft rose-pink muslin, plain and demure. Cally had combed her hair into curls around her face and a loose knot at the back of her head. Picking up a silver-lace shawl, she followed the footman along the passages toward the state room.

Richard was there alone standing by the window, wearing the black velvet evening coat he had worn on the first occasion she had met him. He turned. "Sir Adam will not be joining us, he's feeling a little indisposed after drinking too much maraschino this afternoon while poring over his manuscripts."

"Oh." Her eyes went to the small table by the corner. It had been laid for dinner for two.

"I took the liberty of suggesting we dine here. Three or four at table in that barn of a dining room is bad enough, but only two—"

"Yes."

He handed her a glass of pale sherry. "Unless you would prefer to dine alone, that is."

"To be perfectly honest, I do not know which I would prefer to do."

"Janine, I *did* happen upon something today which would have better been reserved for the bedchamber of a husband and wife!"

"You don't understand at all, do you?"

"I understand that there is obviously a very great deal between you and Mark Talbot."

"I'm very fond of him, it's true."

"I know. I also know that a match between you and him is something your grandfather does not want."

"There is a great deal my grandfather does and does not want, isn't there, Richard? He is doomed to disappointment, however, as we both well know."

"You intend marrying him, then?"

"When I'm face to face with you like this, I'm sorely tempted. *His* company is pleasant—no, *more* than that. I enjoy *his* company."

"And his embraces apparently."

"I have never experienced yours, sir," she retorted.

"True, but then such an experience might prove too overwhelming."

"I doubt it."

The conversation ended there as the doors opened to admit Witherspoon escorting the first course.

Afterward they remained at the table, an ice-bucket containing a bottle of champagne between them. She toyed with the centerpiece of freesias, taking a flower out to smell it.

"You are either pensive, Janine, or exceedingly bored. Which is it?"

She smiled. "Bored? In *your* company? Now, how could that ever be?"

"Unbelievable, I admit."

"You're insufferable."

"Well, you will not have to endure me for a few days, as I must go to York again in the morning."

"Another day's work to stretch to a month?"

"Maybe I exaggerated when I said that. I must go and there *is* a great deal to do there."

"Taverns to visit? Cyprians to call upon? Maybe"— she lowered her voice in mock awe—"maybe even a wicked, low *theater* to sneak into?"

"Would that you were right, but I have solicitors to see, bloodstock to sell, land to view and a court case to attend."

"I would feel sorry for anyone else."

"I can withstand your lack of pity." He poured her another glass of the champagne. "What do you intend doing about Talbot?"

Her dark blue eyes were violet in the candlelight. "Nothing."

"Then what was all that about today? Do you normally caper around in meadows with gentlemen?"

"Are you about to be heavy and boorish again?"

"No. I'm curious."

"Which is said to have killed the cat."

"You don't intend telling me?"

"You *are* persistent, aren't you? Very well. I was enjoying today, being with him, being courted instead of scorned or told off, being liked instead of loathed or at best tolerated. I know he loves me, just as he knows I do not love him. But that does not preclude enjoyment of each other's company. That, Mr. Stuart, was what all *that* was about today."

He looked at her for a moment. "Many marriages are made of a great deal less than that."

"Maybe they are, but any marriage I make will be made of a great deal more. You may relax, Richard, for if curiosity did not kill your cat, that same cat will not be betrayed during your absence by this particular mouse. I shall not be seeing Mark until the night of the ball. But you know, I am not the loose-moraled, flighty piece of muslin you appear to think I am. I am merely capable of wanting to enjoy life occasionally, which trait is no doubt beyond your comprehension."

He took out a cigar. "Do you mind?"

"No."

"It's a fine evening still. Would you like to walk in the gardens?"

"Alone? Or am I to understand that is actually an invitation?"

"If I wanted you out of my sight, you'd be in no doubt. I'm asking you to walk with me; maybe you can help my poor, befuddled brain to comprehend these peculiar traits you appear to suffer from."

Outside it was a magnificent evening. There was hardly any breeze but the warmth in the air was pleasant and not stifling. The sky was a clear, dark turquoise, drifting to primrose and gold where the sun had sunk beyond the western moors. A blackbird was singing somewhere among the trees of Calworth Woods, and the fish in the pools came up to the surface to catch the lazy droning insects. The fading light was draining the blue from the delphiniums and whitening the cream of the rambling roses as Janine and Richard walked slowly along the little paths.

He paused, one foot on the stone edge of a raised pool by a fountain. "You still think you can leave this place, Janine?" He glanced at her as she said nothing.

"You may be Peg Oldfield's daughter in so many ways, but I think you are really more Winterton when it comes down to it."

"Maybe I am, but even a Winterton cannot withstand too many days with incidents like today's. You seem to sweep down from Olympus with thunderbolts and lightning to hurl at me rather too frequently."

"My fury was born of hardly being able to believe my own eyes."

"And the inevitable urge to believe the worst after all! You see? It would *never* work for me to remain here. My nerves would be in tatters after another month of this. And there will be other things to cope with when Lady Serena returns too. No, I may be Winterton, but I'm Peg Oldfield enough to refuse to put up with it."

"All right, all right!" he said, turning to look at her. "I was wrong today. Will that suffice?"

"No. It's condescending! And superior, as usual."

"God above, if I apologize, it's not right. What more can I say, but that I'm sorry about this afternoon?"

She looked up at him. "You can say it as if you mean it for once."

"Janine, I *do* mean it," he said softly. "And if saying it doesn't convince, maybe I must prove it in another way." He pulled her closer and tilted her face toward his. His lips were soft and warm as he kissed her. "I'm sorry, Janine," he murmured. "And now before you kick my shin for being advantage-taking, I shall wish you good night."

He was gone, walking slowly toward the house. She stared after him, her lips burning from that single kiss.

But he had already left Calworth when she went down to the breakfast room the next morning. She did not know how she would have reacted if he had been there. Hiding her love would have been maybe beyond even her acting capabilities this time—

Sir Adam was in grumpy mood, sipping an herb tisane and nibbling cold toast. "I shall never touch maraschino again, so help me, I won't. Damned Devil's brew."

"Until the next time."

"That sort of remark was what greeted me when your grandmother was alive too. Women are unbelievably unsympathetic at times. But every dog has his day, and I have only to wait."

"I shall be most careful not to give you the opportunity of gloating, then," she said, reaching across for the marmalade.

He poured her some coffee. "Richard's gone to York, went at first light."

"Yes."

"Over it now, are you? It seemed to me yesterday that you have a soft heart for Mark Talbot."

She thought for a moment. After his conversation with Richard, perhaps it would be as well to let him think she did indeed care more for Mark. "I'm over Richard, yes. A foolish and momentary deviation into the realms of the ridiculous."

"Oh, well, that's one way of putting it, I suppose. Still, enough of such things. Have you thought of what you will go to the ball as, yet?"

"No."

"Well, you'd best get on with it, time's ticking by. There'll be some really fine get-ups there, you know. Anyway, feel free to go through your grandmother's things in the attic for any fabrics you may take a fancy to."

"I couldn't do that!"

"Why not? Those things are gradually rotting away for no good reason. Catherine wouldn't approve, I'm sure, she was too practical. So, you take a look and see what you can find. Cally Arkwright's a nifty needle-woman, I'm sure, between you, you can come up with something good."

He stirred his tisane for a while. "When first you came here, Janine, you said that you came because of a promise you made to your mother."

"Yes."

"Well, that promise has been kept. What have you decided?"

"I don't know. Oh, please don't be hurt!"

"I'm not hurt, my dear, for I understand. Why should you cope with Serena's huffs and puffs, or with Richard's behavior—whatever that's all about. You should not feel you have to remain here because of me, although I would like that, of course. It's not fair or right of me to expect it of you."

"I love you so, Grandfather."

"Then I'm content. You do as you feel right—as long as it's understood that if you go back to the the-ater, then I expect frequent invitations to stay at—where is it? Lavender Street?"

"Yes. My house is your house, Grandfather. You need no invitation to go there whenever you wish."

He patted her hand. "I will remember. But for the moment, I must go to my manuscripts again."

"What *do* you find to pore over all the time?" She laughed.

"Rude wench, it's a very learned pastime, I'll have you know. I intend gathering all my translations into a very erudite volume. You, in the meantime, can apply yourself to the less taxing occupation of deciding upon your costume for the ball."

"Which puts me firmly in my proper place," she said with a smile.

"Indeed, yes," he said as he went to the door, his cane tapping. "Fancy having the nerve to scoff at my manuscripts!"

Cally sat on the stool, her chin in her hands. "I can't think of anything," she said at last, "not anything *different*."

Janine sighed. "I can't either. Well, what sort of thing do the ladies usually wear for the ball?"

"Lady Serena *always* goes as a goddess or something."

"Heaven forbid," murmured Janine.

"Lady Angela used to dress up in crinnylings."

"Crinolines."

"That's what I said. Crinnylings. She had a green one one year, and a bright red wig with all ringlets hanging down. She carried a basket of oranges and said she was Nell Gwyn or someone."

"Well, I can't think of what to go as," said Janine, getting up and going to the window. "I ought to be able to think of *something*." She smiled wickedly. "I could go as Eve and wear a fig leaf—that'd make them all sit up, eh?"

"Oh, Miss Janine, you *wouldn't!*"

"No, I wouldn't. I'd like to think I had the neck, though."

She looked out the window at the moors shimmering in the heat of the noonday sun. The ball was a week away and she still had no inkling whatsoever of what to wear. It ought to be something *different*, she thought, something no other female head might think of—but what? That was the question. There would the queens, nymphs, goddesses, Spanish ladies, fair damsels of various kinds. What would Peg have worn? Well, Peg would have done something outrageous like dressing as a man, and that would surely not do!

"The Countess of Marcheson went as Marie Antoinette," said Cally suddenly. "She could hardly move in her stays and all that satin. And her wig was so high her neck ached by the end of the ball from just holding her head straight."

Marie Antoinette. Janine stared at the moors thoughtfully. Then she looked at Cally excitedly. "Cally! What else do you think of when you think of Marie Antoinette?"

The maid put a finger to her throat and drew it expressively across the soft skin.

"Precisely! She was beheaded. What if I were to go as Marie Antoinette on her way to the *guillotine?* I could get you to cut my hair all *à la victime,* and wear a white shift!"

"A *shift?*" cried the maid in horror. "But that's not polite, Miss Janine!"

"Why? What can you see through a shift that you can't see through fine muslin?"

"Nothing. But shifts are *under*clothes!"

But Janine was carried by the thought. "Well, we could make one of flowing white linen or something thick and uninteresting. Yes, and I could put a red ribbon around my throat, just like a horrible wound."

"Oo, don't, Miss Janine, you make me feel all funny!"

"What do you think, Cally?"

"Well, I suppose it's unusual."

"Go on, it's a splendid notion and you know it. Right, then, that's it. I shall go as Marie Antoinette on the last day."

"But your lovely hair, Miss Janine, you can't cut it all off like that—"

"Why not? It's the fashion with some folk."

"Aye, but it's not the fashion with *nice* folk."

"Oh, *Cally!*"

The maid grinned then. "Oh, all right, I'll cut it off, but it seems such a shame when it's so lovely like it is."

"And the white cloth?"

"I don't know where that'll come from—"

"Sheets? Old ones?"

"Maybe. I'll have a good look round any road."

"My grandfather said we could use anything we wanted from the trunks in the attic. Maybe there's something up there. Come on."

The attics were warm and stuffy after the sunshine on the past two days, and dust danced in the beams of sun which blazed through the small roof windows.

Cally went to a window and stretched to look out. "You can see almost to Talbot Castle from up here," she said. "And you can see the Dog Stone plain as plain."

Janine stood beside her. "Look how everything's trembling in the heat. It's as if there's a lake or sea or something beyond that hill."

"Ghostie Water," said the maid. "There's a legend that if you can take a drink of the water you'll live forever and be friendly with the little folk."

"Legends!" said Janine, turning away to go into the attic where her grandmother's trunks were. "There are apparently legends to suit everything up here."

"Oh, yes. When you went to Leyworth yesterday you must have seen—"

"Don't tell me. Dragongarth Pool!"

"That's right. Oh, a proper creepy place that is sometimes. Mind, *I* wouldn't mind being there with Lord Talbot to hold my hand."

Janine looked around at her. "Forward hussy," she said.

"I wish I was. I'd maybe have the courage to tek a last fling."

"You make your forthcoming marriage to poor Tom sound like a prison sentence."

"Well, it is in a way. Marriage is if you tek it seriously. That's why you've got to have a good time while you can, when you're not bound by any church-promises."

Janine sat on the nearest trunk, laughing. "If you're

the condemned man, Cally Arkwright, that makes Mark, Lord Talbot, a hearty breakfast!"

They laughed together and then applied themselves to the sorting through of Catherine Winterton's clothes. Henry Winterton's sea chest was still there, still firmly locked. Janine would have liked to see inside, to see her father's things, but her grandfather had never offered and she knew that somehow she would never ask.

Catherine's clothes were rich and beautiful, full skirts of luxurious fabrics, some embroidered, some woven, some plain, some striped. How heavy these garments must have been to wear, thought Janine, glancing down at her own plain muslin gown with its tiny puff sleeves and drawstring beneath the breasts.

"There's nothing 'ere, Miss Janine," said Cally at last. "Not a single thing in white."

"Let's try that last trunk."

The key turned rustily and Cally gasped as Janine drew out the gown which rested there in its neat tissue paper and lavender bags. "Oh, Miss Janine, it's her wedding gown, the one she wears in the portrait in the ballroom. You've maybe not seen it yet. Oh, look at the little pearls and things. Oh, I've never seen anything richer in my life."

The pale primrose material slithered in Janine's hands, the countless folds so small and heavy that they seemed to have a life of their own.

They held it up for a while, speechless at its beauty.

"It makes today's fashions look so plain, doesn't it?" said Janine after a while. "No waists, no full skirts, no endless gathers."

The door opened on the attic stairs and they heard Sir Adam coming up, his cane tapping. He came into the room and saw the gown, and a fond smile came to his face. "Your grandmother looked wonderful that day, Janine, quite wonderful. Did you want to wear it for the ball, then?"

"I—"

"Don't be shy to ask, for if that is what you would like, then please do so. It would give me much pleasure to see it being worn by a Winterton again after all these years. It was only worn once, you know. On our wedding day. The portrait in the ballroom was a little bit deceitful really; the fellow painted the dress when it was hanging on a wooden model, and painted your grandmother when she sat for him another time."

Janine glanced at Cally. To wear a gown like this, so romantically beautiful and magnificent— The maid's eyes shone and she nodded. All thoughts of hair *à la victime* went flying away.

"I'd like to wear it for the ball, Grandfather," said Janine. "I really would."

He smiled. "It's yours then, my dear. It's yours."

------------ *Chapter 21* ------------

The day of the ball dawned bright and clear. But with it came Serena. She arrived back at Calworth at midday, and made a magnificent entrance as Janine and Sir Adam had sat down for luncheon. The house itself was in chaos, with workmen putting up extra lights and galleries around the ballroom. The noise echoed through every room, and together with the constant practicing of the orchestra, Janine's head was ringing into an ache which was not improved by the sight of Serena bearing down upon her across the dining room.

"Ah," said Sir Adam, standing, "there you are at last! Feeling better?"

Serena's sharp eyes went brightly to Janine. "Infinitely," she said. "Where's Richard?"

"York. Are you going to sit down or must I dance about letting my luncheon get cold?"

"I'm sitting down, Adam, don't be impatient. When is Richard returning?"

"By tonight, I trust, otherwise he will miss the ball."

Serena accepted a bowl of brown Windsor soup and her little eyes went toward Janine again. Janine disliked the look in those eyes very much, for it was uncomfortably—triumphant. Yes, that was the word. Serena looked like a victorious general.

Adam sniffed. "Did you enjoy your visit to London?"

"Yes, indeed I did."

"And your sister-in-law, or whoever it was?"

"Eh? Oh, she was well enough when I got there."

"If she was ever ill," he muttered.

"There's more noise here than in a cattle market, Adam. What on earth is going on in the ballroom?"

"The galleries are going up. For the rose petals."

"Oh. That should have been done days ago, not on the actual morning!"

"You were not here to nag me," he replied. "Nor were you here to see that the rose petals were collected. There are fifteen maids and garden boys out there collecting them now."

"Adam, *you* know what has to go into the preparations for this ball as well as I do, so how *I* can be blamed for this chaos, I don't know."

He sniffed again, scowling. "I'd forgotten how prickly mealtimes were when you're around, Serena."

Serena's eyes met Janine's again, and Janine put down her spoon. "Did you have a good journey home, my lady?" She was careful not to say "aunt," anything for a peaceful life—

"Perfect, my dear. Quite perfect." The "my dear" positively dripped with venom. Serena was virtually *purring*.

Janine's discomfort grew as the meal progressed. Serena's attitude felt like a sword of Damocles suspended above her, although why she should think that she could not have said.

At the end of the meal, when Sir Adam was enjoying the brandy with which he liked to sit after his coffee, he looked across to where Serena sat in her favorite seat.

"And are we to take it, sister mine, that you've come back prepared to acknowledge that Janine here is indeed your niece?"

"Why yes, Adam. I accept that she is Henry's child."

"Come to your senses at last, and about time too!"

She made no reply, but asked about her stepson again. "You're sure he'll be back tonight?"

"As sure as anyone can be—I'm not his blasted keeper, woman! He said he'd be back for the ball and so I should imagine that is what he intends. Don't fuss; Calworth Ball will not fail dismally if he is not here."

During the afternoon Serena busied herself with the final arrangements for the great evening, and Janine made one small attempt to ask her if she could do anything to help.

"No, my dear, I'm managing perfectly well without any help, thank you."

Serena handed a waiting footman yet another garland of roses and ribbons. "Not there, you fool, a little further up. That's better. Carry on with them in exactly the same way, if you please."

Janine stood there, undecided. "I feel guilty not doing anything at all."

"Guilty?" purred her aunt. "Now why should you feel guilty, mm? Everything's going very well now that I've picked up the ends Adam managed to drop everywhere."

"Aunt Serena—"

The shrewd eyes swung coldly to her. "Yes?"

"Could we not be a little more friendly? Please?"

"I am being perfectly friendly, my dear."

"I know. I'm sorry. I thought that maybe if we could get on a little better, then life here would be so much nicer. For both of us."

A strange look passed through her aunt's eyes for a moment, and then the previous hard expression returned. "My dear Janine," she said coolly, "you speak as if you intend remaining here *ad infinitum*."

Janine stared at her. "I—"

"Well, we shall see, won't we? My dear." Serena swept past in a rustle of heavy gray brocade.

As the evening approached at last, Janine luxuriated in a scented bath. Her hair had been washed and a conditioner of herbs was soaking into the dark curls as she leaned back in the soapy water. She had left Serena well alone after that. Her aunt might say she believed she had a niece, but that was all. Her dislike was as strong and unbending as ever. Perhaps it would be harder to cope with now, for before an open enmity could be understood, but not this concealed loathing which was there now.

And by tonight there would probably be Richard to face as well. How would *he* be? Was the momentary gentleness of that last evening something which he would prefer to forget? Would he be as aloof and unbelieving as he had been before? She sank deeper into the warm water miserably.

"Miss Janine?"

"Yes, Cally?"

The maid peeped around the lacquered screen with its Chinese figures. "You'd best get out, there's a carriage come already."

"Already?" Janine clambered out of the high bath and took the towel the maid held out for her. "But I thought there was lots of time yet—"

"There is, but some of them have begun to come early. It's Lady Carden."

"Oh, my hair's soaking and will take ages!"

"No, Miss Janine. I've got the fire going, it'll not take long to dress it long and curled like Lady Catherine's portrait. But do hurry!"

The fire crackled and spat and Janine flinched but

remained steadfastly by the heat, rubbing her hair as briskly as she could. When it was almost dry, Cally began to brush and curl it, taking endless time with each thick, raven-colored tress. The curls bounced into place in a mass on the top of her head, and then there were longer, smoother tresses hanging down her back, ending in wispy curls almost at her waist.

"There, what'd I say?" said Cally, putting the hairbrush down and pinning one heavy top curl into place at the back of Janine's head. "Now this jeweled comb Sir Adam said went with the dress. Oh, Miss Janine, you look grand."

"And very hairy," said Janine. "It's very odd to be without a knot or something to make it look neat."

"It's how she had it in the portrait, and *I* think it's grand. Now for the stays."

"Oh, dear."

"You'll never get into the dress without them."

"I know."

The stays felt tighter and tighter as the maid laced them around Janine's already slender body. The wedding gown slithered softly and heavily around her waist as Cally fastened it, and then brought the separate bodice with its stiff boning and low, square neckline. When a few minutes later Janine looked at her reflection in the cheval mirror, it was not because of the stays that she held her breath. The gown was more beautiful than she had thought before, its little gathers and tiny pearls so perfectly stitched that everything about it was perfection. Its delicate primrose color made her dark hair look blue-black in the fading evening light, and with only the jeweled comb to sparkle and flash, she felt that she looked the epitome of the fashion of forty years earlier.

The door opened suddenly and Serena came in, wearing a brief black gauzy gown studded with glittering sequins. A golden quiver was in one hand, and a golden bow in the other, and she stood obviously aside for Cally to go out. The hennaed hair was redder than ever somehow tonight as she looked at Janine.

"So, Catherine's wedding gown. You take my breath away at times, missy. Well, I am here to warn you that if you come down to that ballroom tonight, you must expect to hear things said which will not please you. No, they will not please you at all."

Janine stared at her. "What things?"

"Oh, come now. I think you know already what I'm talking about and I don't propose to waste my breath repeating them to you. You are Henry's child and therefore, I suppose, entitled to address me as your aunt. But you have no right to be here. I intended saying something earlier at luncheon, but Richard was not there and so I waited. He has returned now, and I shall go ahead with my original plan and expose you for the opportunist I still believe you to be. No, I shall not explain myself further, I just warn you that you would be better advised not coming down tonight. Good evening, Janine."

Janine remained silent, her heart thundering and her mouth dry. Her aunt turned and left the quiet room. Janine looked at her reflection again. Not go down? But what could Serena have to say that could possibly be true?

Her fan lay on the dressing table beside her tasseled dance card. She looked at her reflection again, and held her head up. There weren't any threats which Peg Oldfield would have succumbed meekly to! None. She pulled on her white gloves, picked up the fan and card and swept from the room to go down to the ball.

Chapter 22

The ballroom lay at the back of the house, a huge room the height of the first two stories, and stretching for a third of the house's length. The tall windows looked out onto a terrace where hundreds of ornamental shrubs had been placed in pots and where strings of lanterns swayed in the slight summer-evening breeze. But inside everything glittered and sparkled. Many extra chandeliers had been suspended from the high ceiling, and the countless hundreds of candles were reflected in the polished parquet flooring. The gallery had been decorated with the garlands and behind it, hidden from view, were the many buckets of rose petals which were to be thrown down by servants when the last dance was played. At the far end of the gold, white and marble room was the orchestra, surrounded by ferns and palms and with crimson drapes hanging elegantly behind them, the Winterton arms emblazoned at the top where the gathered, fringed hangings came together.

As Janine reached the top of the wide, shallow steps which led down to the floor from the rear of the vestibule, she saw that already there were quite a number of guests there. The orchestra was playing a mazurka as her name was announced, and she began the descent, knowing that many curious, interested looks were turned in her direction.

Her grandfather, resplendent in his Charles II costume, turned to greet her at his place at the foot of the steps. "Ah, there you are, my dear, and how very lovely you look." He pointed up at the portrait of Catherine Winterton in its place of honor on the wall opposite the windows. "Replace her fair hair with your dark hair, my dear, and it could be you up there, could it not?"

She looked, and it was indeed almost like looking at herself. But she smiled at him. "Except that she was probably a lot thinner than I am, for I can hardly breathe."

"Nor could she, my dear, nor could she. Oh, dear, here comes Serena, and she looks *thunderous*—I wonder what can have gone wrong. Good evening, Serena."

Serena came slowly down the steps, glaring angrily at Janine who merely raised a defiant chin and stared her out.

"Good evening, Adam. My dear."

"You make your greeting sound like Mr. Justice de Courtais pronouncing sentence of death, Serena. Is something the matter? Moon goddesses are supposed to be serene—like your name—not black-scowled and ominous."

"In good time I will explain," she said mysteriously, glancing witheringly at Janine, before accepting a glass of champagne from the tray held by the silent footman.

"Where's Richard? He *is* here, isn't he?"

Serena nodded. "He's here and will be down directly. I left him quibbling at wearing a periwig. I told him that an eighteenth-century rake would hardly have short hair and no wig, but I doubt if the wig will be on view down here tonight by the time he's finished."

Sir Adam chuckled. "Well, no doubt he'll be passable as whatever it is. An eighteenth-century *rake*, you say?"

"Yes, complete with satins and buckled shoes."

For a moment Adam's attention was drawn away, and Serena stepped closer to Janine. "I warned you, missy, and believe me it was for your own sake that I did so."

"I choose not to take heed, my lady," replied Janine. "Do your worst, whatever it is, and I will remain here and face you out."

"I think then that you will wish you had not. However, the choice is yours."

Serena moved on to mingle with the guests, leaving Janine to stand with her grandfather, greeting each new arrival. There were several harlequins, a Queen Elizabeth, a bear who swore like a trooper and complained at being hot to boiling already and he hadn't finished his first glass, a Queen Guinevere, three Lord Nelsons, a Negress with unlikely fair hair and four fairy queens of varying girths. After a while she found that she no longer noticed the costumes, and hardly paid attention to the names of those she was introduced to. She kept glancing up the steps to see if Richard was coming.

Mark arrived before Richard. He was announced and came down the steps, a magnificent figure in medieval velvets. His doublet was of dull green and his hose of dark blue, and he had a fur-trimmed crimson hat with a long scarf which was wound loosely around his neck.

Sir Adam was thoughtful. "Let me guess. I know. King Arthur."

"No. Wrong century."

"Which century then?"

Mark smiled. "The fifteenth."

"Oh, damn me, I don't know. Richard the Second."

"Try his cousin. I'm supposed to be Henry the Fourth."

"You're not fat enough, dear boy. Better tell them you're Richard. Mind, I suppose *he* got fat in the end too, come to think of it. Still, you look splendid, my boy. Take Janine off my hands for a dance, will you? She's been dithering around at my side for so long she's making me jittery. Go on, go on with you, my dear. It's time Serena took a turn at this caper here. Serena?"

He was gone, catching a glimpse of his sister somewhere among the crowd.

Mark took Janine's hand. "You look beautiful, Janine," he said, leading her onto the floor for a cotillion. She presented him with her lace handkerchief as she curtseyed at the beginning of the dance, moving on in the intricate, slow steps, accepting a favor from one of the Lord Nelsons and handing it on to an Oliver Cromwell. By the end of the dance, as was designed, she was opposite Mark again, and her own handkerchief was returned to her. Another mazurka followed, and she remained with Mark, glancing from time to time toward Serena at the foot of the stairs. Whatever her aunt intended saying tonight, she was in no hurry to put her unfortunate niece out of her misery.

And then Richard arrived. He wore a pale blue satin coat with low patch pockets from which protruded floppy handkerchiefs, a dark blue brocade waistcoat which came to well below his waist in the fashion of the middle of the previous century, and heavy lace spilled from his cuffs. He wore oyster-colored breeches which ended just below his knee, white stockings and black shoes with large golden buckles. And there was no sign of the wig which should have accompanied such an outfit.

"He's cheating," said Mark. "No wig, no powder and no patches. He's cried off going all out."

"He looks as if we're lucky he's wearing what he is."

"I don't think masquerades are in Richard Stuart's line somehow. He sneaked away on some excuse the week before last year's and didn't come back in time. Still, he's obviously decided to grace the evening with his presence this year," said Mark, losing interest.

"I hope you and he won't—"

"Throw down gauntlets all over the place? I doubt it. Well, you're causing a stir, aren't you? I've been watching, and nearly everyone in the room is eyeing you, either from behind fans, through lorgnettes or merely staring quite openly."

"Don't, you make me quite nervous."

"Why? You're the most beautiful woman here, and the men desire you and the women envy you. You should be lording it over the lot of them."

"You're very good for my morale, Mark Talbot."

"Good. Because it seems to me that you're upset about something tonight. Richard?"

"No, I haven't spoken to him since he came back."

"Serena then."

"Yes. But, Mark, I'd really rather not talk about it."

"Very well, I'll desist this instant."

They danced on, and as Janine turned once, she looked across the room straight into Richard's eyes. He inclined his head and she did the same.

When the mazurka came to an end and Mark was about to lead her from the floor again, Richard pushed through the crowds. "Ah, Mark, I claim your partner from you, to allow you time to recover from leaping around in those furs and velvets."

Mark gave him a faint smile and bowed, giving him Janine's hand. But Richard led her across the dance floor and out onto the terrace where there were very few people.

"I'm told by Sir Adam that Serena has accepted that you are her niece."

"Apparently."

He looked closely at her. "What's going on, then?"

"I beg your pardon?"

"She's got her enigmatic, scheming look on—I've seen it enough times before to recognize it by now. So, do you know what's going on?"

She looked at him and then away, shaking her head.

He put a hand to her chin and made her look at him. "Is this a belated kick on the shin?"

"No, Richard. I don't know what she's going to do, merely that she's going to do something to expose me for the opportunist she still believes I am." She bit her lip and looked determinedly away again to hide the tenseness which she knew was in her face. "She warned me not to come down to the dance tonight."

"I'll get to the bottom of it."

"No, leave it be. Leave it be, Richard. Let her do it, whatever it is, for I have nothing to hide. I am what I say I am and that is all I have ever claimed."

"Janine, I believe you. But is there anything else in your past which she may have discovered during her stay in London? Anything at all?"

She looked swiftly at him, raising her head. "*No!* I have not left my illegitimate children behind me, nor my string of lovers, Richard Stuart! Nor have I gambling debts of great magnitude, nor a drunken husband. In short, I am boringly innocent of anything!" She turned and gathered her full skirts, leaving him standing by the balustrade.

There was a lull in the dancing when she went back into the ballroom, and the babble of conversation drowned the soft music of the orchestra. Many guests were helping themselves to the wondrous selection of foods on the white-clothed tables lining the inner wall.

Mark caught her hand, smiling. "Yet another tiff?"

"Yes."

"Take a calming drink with me then, for I am much more amenable company."

She smiled. "Yes, you are."

He put a hand to her waist as they walked to where the huge punch bowl stood, and he ladled two tiny cups, handing her one. "The next time he butts in, then, I shall refuse to part with you. Ah, good evening, Judge de Courtais, I trust your courts haven't been too full of late?"

The judge was a fat, squat man dressed as a sailor, but the blue and white stripes of his ragged shirt did nothing to improve his round shape. "Full? Bless me, I think there's more scoundrels about these days than ever before. Poachers, footpads, highwaymen, thieves and cutthroats. There's none of us safe in our beds these days. Begging your pardon, Miss Winterton, I don't mean to frighten you."

"Not at all, sir," she said smiling, but from the corner of her eye she saw Serena maneuvering her grandfather toward them. There was something about her aunt which told her that the moment had come and Serena was about to carry out her plan.

"Ah, Judge de Courtais," beamed her aunt. "How very fortunate a moment to come upon you."

"Eh? Oh. Yes."

Sir Adam nodded as Mark offered him some of the punch. "Going well, ain't it. I'll get them to make some more of this brew, eh, Talbot?"

"It's very potent."

"I intended it to be." Sir Adam laughed. "If you want an evening to go well, you must fill it to the very gills with alcoholic beverages of one sort or another, then you can sit back and watch the fun. God above, it's hot under this wig; you were sensible not to wear one, Richard."

Janine looked behind and saw that Richard had indeed joined them. Mark still had his hand on her waist, and he drew her closer. "Sip up," he whispered, "you look as frightened as a rabbit. Are you feeling unwell maybe?"

"No—no, I'm quite all right." She spoke to him, but it was at Serena that she was looking.

Serena singled the judge out again. "And is it not wonderful, sir, that my brother should find that he has a grand-daughter after all this time?"

"Yes, indeed—and so very pretty a gel, eh?" The judge beamed at Janine.

"But tell me," went on Serena, in a voice calculated to attract the attention of all those close by, "would not my nephew Henry Winterton have had to *marry* Janine's mother for Janine to call herself Winterton?"

"Er—" The judge stared at her, clearing his throat and glancing at Sir Adam who remained motionless. Janine leaned a little closer to Mark, who tightened his arm around her waist. Richard took a glass of champagne from the tray a footman was carrying past, and he thrust it into Serena's hand.

"I think, my lady, that this shall be the beginning and *end* of this conversation, don't you?" he said quietly.

The judge closed his eyes with relief, but Serena was not done yet. "No, Richard, it is not the end. I asked the judge a question and I still await his answer. Is Janine entitled to call herself Winterton when her mother was not married to Henry?"

Janine looked at her aunt. "But there *was* a marriage, and I have the certificate!"

"There was a mock marriage, my dear, with one of Henry's friends dressed as the vicar of St. Bartholomew's. Your mother was duped—possibly. She certainly was *not* Henry Winterton's wife!"

The silence in the ballroom was awful, and Janine looked helplessly around the sea of faces. "You're lying, I know you are—" she whispered, gazing at Serena again.

"I can prove it, my dear. You are Henry's child—his *bastard!*"

Sir Adam remained silent, and Richard stared at the huge punch bowl. Janine looked at her grandfather, wanting him to look at her, but he did not move. If ever there had been a moment in Janine's life when she was Peg Oldfield's actress daughter, it was now. She held her head up as she turned away, her pattering steps the only sound in the quiet ballroom. Her full, heavy skirts dragged behind her as she went up the steps and out into the vestibule beyond.

Richard glanced uncertainly at Sir Adam who still had said nothing, and then he looked at Serena. "That was badly done, madam!" he said coldly. "And I'm ashamed to be your stepson." Then he followed Janine.

But outside in the vestibule there was no sign of her. He went to the open front doors and looked out at the driveway where the many carriages were drawn up in a seemingly endless line. He looked all around, but she was nowhere to be seen, and so he turned to go up the stairs to her room.

Cally was sitting by the lamp, stitching a torn petticoat, and she stood nervously as he came in.

"Master Richard?"

"Did Miss Winterton come in here?"

"No, Master Richard. Isn't she at the ball with everyone?"

"No, Cally, she is not." He went to the window, but the park was dark and he couldn't see anything beyond the light thrown by the lanterns on the balustrade of the terrace.

He sighed. Where could she have gone—? His eyes went to the black moors beyond.

Chapter 23

Dawn was softening the eastern horizon and only one carriage remained in the drive when Richard and Mark came into the library where Serena and Sir Adam sat alone and silent.

Sir Adam looked at the two men as they came down the steps. "Did you find her?"

"No," said Richard. "I've set some men to go out on the moor as soon as there's light enough to see by. God above, Serena, that was the work of a first-class she-cat! Why on earth did you choose to do it that way?"

Serena folded and unfolded her hands uncomfortably. "To expose her with the maximum of effect."

"Well, you certainly did that! Except that the whole thing came as a great shock to her as well! She didn't come here to Calworth knowing that!"

Serena looked helplessly at him. "I was not to know that. As far as I was concerned—"

"As far as you were concerned, madam, she forced her way in here and *you* did not like it!"

"She was going to take what should have been yours!"

Richard glanced at Sir Adam. "I seem to have been

195

saying a great deal about all this, Sir Adam. Have *you* nothing to say?"

The old man nodded. "Mark, my boy, in that small cupboard over there you will find not only a bottle of cognac and some glasses, but also a book. Will you give me the book and pour us all some cognac?"

"Yes, Sir Adam." Mark opened the cupboard and took out the old red leather book, and handed it to the old man.

"This is my son Henry's diary," said Sir Adam, opening it, "and these entries are for those of October and November 1787. I have read this book from beginning to end since Janine came here, and I had never done that before—because I could not bring myself to. But had I done so, I would have known that I had a grandchild. What Serena said tonight was true—and I knew it. Henry *did* fake that marriage to poor Peg Oldfield. But what Serena did *not* discover was the fact that my son had a guilty conscience over what he had done, especially as he realized Peg was expecting his child. He righted the wrong, Serena, by marrying her again. In the same church a month later, with the real vicar in attendance this time. Peg was ill when she gave the certificate to Janine, she produced the wrong certificate. The real one is still in her house in London, probably—I don't know. But whatever the reason for the incorrect certificate coming into Janine's hands, it makes no difference to the facts. Janine is my legitimate granddaughter, and she is still my heir, no matter what." Sir Adam closed the book softly. "He left England shortly after the last entry in this book, and within a day or so he was dead. Serena, if anything happens to Janine because of your spiteful interference, I shall never forgive you, do you hear me? Never."

Serena stared at him, and then drank the cognac Mark had given her, in one large mouthful. "I thought she was a scheming opportunist," she whispered, "truly

I thought she was—I did it because it seemed the best and only thing to do. It *wasn't* spite, Adam. Richard—you must believe me—"

Richard took a long and heavy breath. "Well, it wasn't for the best, was it? And now we have to find her."

Mark nodded. "I'll help."

"Maybe if you went back to Talbot Castle—" said Richard. "For it could be that she's gone there."

"Very well, I'll go now." Mark put down his glass, looking around at the others. "But you all share the guilt over Janine. Lady Serena's share we know already. You, Richard Stuart, could have made things a great deal easier for her had you but tried. And you, Sir Adam, did not have to remain so horribly silent in the ballroom, did you? That silence must have seemed to her like the ultimate condemnation."

Sir Adam nodded slowly. "I know it, my boy—I surely know it."

Mark inclined his head and left the library. He went through the quiet house to the hallway and out into the pale, clear dawn. He heard the party of searchers ride out from the stableyard, and watched them ride past his solitary, waiting landau, down the driveway toward Calworth Woods. He looked at the purple and red pagoda, its dragons shining brightly in the first rays of the morning sun. Its chimes were tinkling gently in the small breeze, and the sound carried faintly to where he stood.

With a heavy sigh he went down the steps then to the landau, and the footman jumped down to pull out the iron steps for him. He climbed in and sat down—to find himself looking into Janine's large eyes.

"Don't say anything, Mark," she pleaded in a whisper, "just let me go to Talbot with you. *Please*, Mark!"

"But they're all out looking for you, and besides, there's no need. Your aunt was only partly right, there *was* a real wedding afterward, Janine. Sir Adam knows all about it because it's in your father's diary."

"I can't face them," she said after a moment. "I still can't face them. Not after all this. Not anymore." Her hand crept into his.

He caught it quickly and went to sit beside her as the landau turned slowly in the driveway, maneuvering around the fountain. As the team gathered to a smart trot, and the landau began to sway, Janine turned to him suddenly, flinging her arms around his neck as she began to cry. He held her tightly, his cheek resting against her soft, dark hair.

"Don't cry, sweetheart," he murmured. "Come on, now, mm?" He put a hand to her chin and smiled into her tear-stained face.

"I can't help it, Mark."

"Is the unhappiness so bad then?"

"Yes."

"But you're legitimate, Janine. Nothing's changed."

"Everything's changed really. Because I have. I know I must get away from Richard, Mark. I can't live at Calworth anymore, for I love him too much, and he—well, he is indifferent. It's not fair to turn to you, but—"

He kissed her cheek gently. "I will always be here for you to turn to, Janine, no matter what the circumstances. I at last admit defeat, though. So you are coming to Talbot. Then what shall you do?"

"Go back to London."

"Dressed like that?"

"No. Dressed in Angela's clothes."

He studied her face. "Take what you want. And you shall travel in style in this ornate drag." He pushed a stray curl back from her forehead. "God above, how Stuart can be immune to you I shall never understand."

She woke in a strange bed. The room was circular, plastered and painted with bright tapestrylike pictures of ladies and knights, caparisoned horses and hawks. Above, the chandelier was suspended from an ancient wooden ceiling, the candles fixed firmly in black wrought-iron holders. The furniture was of old, dark oak, and the bed in which she lay was heavy and large, its hangings woven with Talbot hounds in silver on a blue background. She lay there listening to the sounds from outside. A horse neighing, hounds baying in the kennels, a man shouting and a maid singing. Sunshine was streaming through the tiny windows of the tower room, and apart from the soreness of her eyes to remind her, the terrible moments of the ball at Calworth might never have been on this pleasant, warm morning.

She slipped from the bed, picking up Mark's dressing gown. His nightshirt was huge, its sleeves hanging beyond the tips of her fingers so that she had to roll it up to her elbows. The dressing gown dragged behind her as she left the room and made her way down the curling stone steps to the floor below.

Mark was awake, sipping coffee from his breakfast tray as he stood by the window. He smiled as she came into his room. "Good morning."

"Good morning."

"Stuart's still got half of Calworth out looking for you. I've been watching. See? Riding along that top ridge, do you see them?"

She stood beside him, watching the distant horsemen. "Mark, you said last night that I could use Angela's things and go in your landau?"

"Yes. But you shall not travel alone, I shall go with you."

"No. No, I shall go by myself."

He cupped her chin in his hands. "You aren't to be trusted out alone. I fear you'd never reach London," he teased.

"I want to go back alone, Mark."

"To the stage, after all?"

"Yes."

"I don't like letting you go at all, and especially all alone. Janine, I love you very, very much. Stay here. With me."

"I—"

"I'm not propositioning you, I want to marry you."

She put her hands over his, shaking her head. "Thank you for asking me. I take it as the very greatest compliment, Mark."

"We could do very well together, you and I, Janine."

"I know. But you deserve a wife who will give you all her love. I could never do that." She slipped her arms around his neck and stretched up to kiss him. "I love you very much, Mark, but it's the wrong kind of love."

He smiled. "I know. Damn it."

She moved away, picking up the coffee pot and sniffing the contents. "It smells good."

He handed her his cup. "When do you intend leaving, then?"

"After breakfast."

"So quickly?"

"Yes. I must make the break as swiftly and finally as I can, while I am feeling as strongly as I do now. If I stay here, I'll weaken and feel guilty about my grandfather, and then I'll go to see him—and maybe be persuaded to remain. I will leave Yorkshire today."

He nodded. "I don't like you traveling alone, though."

"Please, Mark."

"Very well, but my coachman will have the strictest instructions to watch over you."

She smiled. "I will wear collar and chain if it will make you feel happier."

"That's better," he said, returning the smile. "A little of the old Janine again."

"Peg always said that great performers know how to present a brave face to the world."

"Your mother seems to have had a saying to fit every situation."

She looked from the window across the moors. "She did," she said softly, "and she needed them."

Wearing a purple-and-white-striped gown and purple spencer she had sorted from the row of wardrobes in Angela's old rooms, Janine tied on the straw bonnet and nodded as the maid asked her if she wanted only those things she had laid out on the bed to be packed into the hand case. "Yes. Just enough to see me on the journey to London."

She looked at her full-length reflection in the gold-edged mirror opposite. Her eyes looked dark and tired, and her face was tense and pale, but if she held her head proudly and smiled— Picking up the white kid gloves, she left Angela's room and went down through the castle to the courtyard where the landau was waiting.

But as she came out into the sunshine, she saw a second carriage drawn up, and there, talking with Mark, was Serena. Janine froze, and turned to go back inside, but she was too late and Serena saw her.

"Janine?"

Slowly Janine turned. "Yes?"

Serena patted Mark's arm and came toward her. "I guessed that you would be here, and so I came alone."

"Have you some other tasteful morsel to impart, then?"

Serena lowered her eyes for a moment. "No, my dear, I've come to try to make up to you for what I did. It was unforgivable, I know, but if you could find it in your heart to feel a little kindness toward me? I did not think—or I thought too much, maybe. And in the end I was wrong anyway. I'm so very sorry for my behavior, Janine, so very, very sorry. I've hurt you, and hurt Adam, and am now hurt myself, and it's all my own doing. I'm not a woman who's used to apologizing, and maybe I'm not doing it very well—"

"You are doing it very well indeed, Aunt Serena." Janine looked into the older woman's unhappy face and couldn't dislike her anymore. She smiled and took her aunt's hands. "One day I will come back to Calworth maybe, to see you and my grandfather."

"Come now."

"No. Not now. Not for a long while. It's best if I go back to the life I wanted before."

"How can it be for the best? Your grandfather loves you and wants you there, and I want so much to make up to you for what I've done. We all want you back."

"All? There are three of you there who matter, Aunt Serena. You and my grandfather I know about. But what of the third person?"

"Richard? But *Richard* doesn't want you to go!" said Serena in surprise.

"I know, and that's the whole of the trouble really—he's indifferent about whether I go or stay. He could not care less where I was."

Serena stared at her then as she realized the truth. "Richard?" she said at last, glancing at Mark. "But I thought—"

"That I was in love with Mark? No, Aunt Serena, I've loved Richard from the first moment I met him. That's why I have to go now. But I beg of you, don't say anything to him, will you? There's no need for him ever to know. When you get back to Calworth, just tell my grandfather that I love him and that I will come again one day."

"I will tell him."

"Don't let him send anyone after me."

"If that is your wish."

Janine saw the tears shining in her aunt's eyes and she flung her arms around her. "Thank you for coming to talk to me," she whispered.

"I had to, Janine. I have never in my life felt more ashamed or been more ostracized than I am now. Shall I have your things sent after you? Including Lord Wolfe's check?"

"Yes."

Serena smiled. "You, Janine, are doing exactly as your mother did before you, aren't you? You are determined to succeed, and just as determined that you shall do it without the Wintertons."

"Not the Wintertons, Aunt Serena. This time it's without a Stuart."

Janine went to Mark, slipping her arms around him and holding him tightly for a moment. "Thank you, Mark."

"You could still stay and make an honest man of me."

She smiled, and he embraced her for a long time. "Good luck, Janine."

She climbed into the landau and she didn't look back as it rattled over the drawbridge and out onto the moorland track.

Chapter 24

It was raining in London as the landau pulled up at the back of the theater. Janine sat back, looking at the old building for a long while, remembering the last occasion she had arrived here after a long journey. It had been raining then too—

The footman opened the door. "Shall we wait, Miss Winterton?"

"If you please."

Steam rose from the sweating team and their glossy coats were travel-stained. Their glittering harness jingled as they stamped and tossed their heads, and Janine looked back at them as she reached the stage door. The Talbot badge was embossed on the side of the landau. Perhaps she was a fool not to accept Mark. Would she ever find a man who loved her more, or whom she felt so warmly toward? Was a surly, arrogant Scotsman worth all this heart-searching and unhappiness? She pulled the bell and heard its remembered sound rattling inside the building.

"Yes?"

"It's me, Dickon. Janine."

"Miss Jan!" He flung open the door, his arms wide

as he hugged her. "Oh, come in, come in! It's good to see you."

She hugged him, smiling. "It's good to be welcomed so grandly!"

"You'll always be welcome here, Miss Jan. Dobby's here this afternoon, she don't come that often no more, not since— Well, she said that tending anyone else after Peg was just not the same, if you know what I mean."

"I know, Dickon."

"Is this just a quick visit then?" he said, leading her through the theater toward Peg's dressing room.

"Maybe. I thought maybe Mr. Stanleigh might be interested in giving me a contract."

The doorman halted, turning. "*Interested?* He'd turn a cartwheel to get Peg Oldfield's daughter. Not like the grand life, then?"

She smiled. "Oh, I liked it well enough, Dickon, but there were complications which made coming back here a much more pleasing notion than remaining there."

"Well, Yorkshire's loss is London's gain. Mr. Stanleigh's coming later to see some composer or other who reckons to have the niftiest thing in new musical plays."

"Don't they all?"

"Endlessly. Still, maybe this one's *the* one, eh? Well, here we are." He pushed open the door.

Dobby was sitting on Peg's old sofa, and she stared speechlessly at Janine, getting up then and running to hug her, and burst into tears at the same time.

"Oh, Dobby, Dobby, don't cry," said Janine, holding the thin, shaking body for a moment.

"I was *just* thinking about the past, and you walked in— It was—it was like seeing a ghost," muttered the dresser, searching in her reticule for a handkerchief.

Janine looked around the room. Ghost? Maybe there

was a ghost here. The room was just as if Peg were still there, not a thing had been touched. The pots of makeup were as she left them, some open, some closed, some almost new, others almost finished. Above the dressing table the wigs still hung, and all around the walls the costumes Peg had worn and made famous. No one had touched them—

Dobby smiled. "No one would dare to move them, Miss Jan, not even Stanleigh himself."

Dickon touched Janine's arm. "I'll see as you're told the moment he gets here, Miss Jan."

"Stanleigh?" asked Dobby after the doorman had gone. "What'd you want to see that penny-pinching old ratbag for?"

"Penny-pinching old ratbag? Well, really, Dobby."

"That's behind his back." The dresser grinned. "To his face it's, *'Yes, sir, no, sir, three bags full sir.'*"

"I want to know if he'll offer me a contract, Dobby."

The dresser smiled. "He will. And you'll be wanting a dresser."

"*If* I get a contract," said Janine, sitting down on the battered, old red velvet sofa.

"There's no ifs about it, you'll get one." Dobby sat beside her, taking her hand. "What's wrong?"

"Nothing."

"Oh, come on, you can't fool old Dobby. You're your mother's image, Miss Jan, and I can tell there's something wrong just by looking. Why've you come back?"

"I suffer from my mother's execrable taste in men, Dobby."

"Ah. An unhappy love affair?"

"No, Dobby, a nonexistent love affair."

"And you're running away back to all this?"

"Yes. I suppose I am."

"Then you'll need every ounce of talent you have, because you'll be giving only half of yourself to the stage, Miss Jan. Give your *all* and you'll be as brilliant as your mother was, more brilliant maybe. Peg had style, Miss Jan, and a personality which filled the whole auditorium because she *wanted* to be there, to dominate everything. It was what drove her, what kept her at the pinnacle. Take away a sliver or two of that and a little of the sparkle goes too. You'll need luck, Miss Jan, and endless willpower. Have you got that?"

"I think so, Dobby."

The dresser took her hand gently. "And if this man you love should come for you, you'd leave it all in the snap of a finger?"

"Yes. But, I hasten to add, there is not the slightest likelihood of that happening, Dobby, for he is supremely indifferent to me."

"The fellow's a fool, then, and not worth any misery. Now then, shall I brew a pot of Peg's Pekoe?"

"You've still got it?"

"Of course."

"Did he offer a *good* contract?" demanded Dobby as she and Dickon waited for Janine to speak.

"Yes," said Janine, sitting down weakly. "He—he offered me *Peg's* contract. Down to the last detail."

They stared, and then Dobby nodded. "Aye, well, reckon he would an' all, for you're worth it to any theater in London."

"She worked all her life to get to that contract, Dobby. I don't deserve to walk in and pick up the same terms."

"He knows that if you go elsewhere he's lost the biggest name London will see for a long time," said the dresser, nudging Dickon.

"Oh," he said, "yes, we've a celebration to get on with then, eh?" He produced a bottle of champagne.

"Oh, *Dickon!*" cried Janine, clapping her hands. "Just what I feel in need of!"

"It ain't cold, but then what's a lump of ice between friends, eh?" The cork popped and the champagne fizzed out over the dressing room.

They laughed, holding up Peg's teacups for their drinks.

When they were sitting down again, Dobby asked Janine if the manager had had any particular play in mind for her.

"Well, he's got one idea and one only at the moment. That I must emulate Peg. I'm to be billed as Peg's daughter, the main attraction in a memorial to her."

"A memorial?" asked Dickon. "But they've had one!"

"I gathered that. But this one is to be nothing but a continuous performance of Peg's most loved songs. I'm to sing them as she sung them, and I'm to wear the costumes she wore. In other words, I'm to *be* Peg Oldfield again."

"Stanleigh don't miss a trick," said Dobby sagely. "It can't fail, can it? A show like that and a name like yours. You'll set London alight, Miss Jan. Like I said earlier, you can do it, for you've the talent and more. But it's the *will* which'll be the decider in the end."

Janine looked at the dresser and nodded. "I know, Dobby. I know."

The landau turned into Lavender Street, splashing through the puddles collected in the ruts in the road. Janine looked up at the houses as they passed the rain-drenched windows. How close together they were after the wide grandeur of Calworth, and how the streets seemed to interweave and close in the further into the city you went. It was all almost overpowering, as were the noise and bustle even late in the evening when the light was fading. Children ran and played in the rain, screaming and shouting, and a dog began to bark before a watchman threw a stone at it and it ran howling away, its tail between its legs.

But outside number seventeen it was quiet. She looked up at the house. It should be like coming home, but it wasn't. If Peg had been there waiting then things would have felt different, but now—

The footman opened the door for her.

"You'll find the mews around the back," she said, "and you will find all the accommodation and food you need in the house."

"Yes, Miss Winterton."

She watched the landau sway on its final few yards of journey to the mews lane. It turned and was gone from sight, and suddenly the street was very quiet and empty. The children had gone, shooed away by an indignant old gentleman in a bath-chair, and there was only the sound of the gray rain as it splashed and bubbled on pavements and rooftops high above. The trees dripped dismally, and even the sea gulls swooping and wheeling in the heavy sky were silent for once.

She turned the bell and waited for Carter. Steps came along the tiled hall and the door opened. She turned, and looked straight into Richard's face.

"Good evening, Janine," he said, standing aside for her to enter.

"How—?"

"I posted down with all due haste," he said, "intending to overtake you, but then Talbot's drag is more nifty than I gave him credit for."

"Why did you come, Richard? Were you bored with no one to be unpleasant to?" she said, taking off her gloves and bonnet and going into the drawing room, her head spinning with the shock of suddenly seeing him again when she thought him so many miles away.

"I came to persuade you to come back to Calworth."

"For my grandfather?"

"For him, yes. And for Serena."

"And for yourself?" She turned to look at him, wondering if Serena had kept her promise or if maybe she had told him after all.

"I did not ever want you to go, Janine."

"Ah, but did you ever want me to stay?"

"Yes, you know that I did."

She looked around the drawing room, shivering. "Where are the servants?"

"I gave them the rest of the day off."

"Oh, *did* you?"

He smiled. "I have an air of authority which they find difficult to resist."

"I'll warrant. So, there is no one to prepare a meal?"

"I'll take you out to dine."

She smiled. "Maybe I was looking forward to a quiet meal at home."

"Were you?"

"Yes."

"Then I will send out to have Kandari send a *cordon bleu* repast here."

"Maybe too I wanted to dine alone, or had *that* not occurred to you?"

He folded his arms, leaning back against a table watching her. "And *did* you?"

"Not anymore."

"Ah, then my company is not totally abhorrent to you?"

She flushed a little. "No."

He glanced at the windows which were awash with rain, making the oil lamps outside look distorted. "I take it you've been to the theater—you must have been or you would have been here sooner."

"Yes."

"And?"

"And I have a contract."

"Signed?"

"No, not until eleven o'clock tomorrow."

"Then I have until then to dissuade you from signing."

"All night?"

"If it takes that long, then yes. Scots may be taciturn, Janine, but when necessary they become very garrulous."

"Richard, if this is just a gesture, a belated attempt at being pleasant because you have a conscience—"

"I have no conscience, Janine."

"No, I was obviously assuming a little too much there, wasn't I?" she replied, unbuttoning her spencer and putting it over a chair.

"What I did I would do all over again."

"How very pleasing to know it."

"Because had I not behaved as I did, I would not have had my eyes opened as to your true worth, Janine. You have more spirit in your little finger than any other woman I've met, more beauty and more charm too. There's a fire in you a man would not mind being burned on."

"A man like you maybe?" she asked lightly.

"Aye, why not a man like me? I find you very desirable, Janine, too desirable, I think."

She stared at him, wanting to believe him and yet, at the back of her mind, she had the suspicion that maybe Serena *had* told him and that he was using that knowledge to persuade her to go back. "Aunt Serena told you, didn't she?" she said suddenly, to force his hand. "I made her promise not to—"

"Serena? What's Serena got to do with this? She's said nothing to me. What *could* she say anyway?"

"I—"

"Well? It must have been important."

"It was." She bit her lip and turned away, running her fingers over the carved marble vines decorating the fireplace. "But it doesn't matter—"

He came closer. "Janine, I had a reason for dismissing your servants tonight, a purely selfish one, of course. They will not now be there to witness a vanquished Scot slinking from the house with a black eye and a sore shin."

She turned. "Vanquished?"

"I want you back at Calworth, Janine, because, damn it, I can't bear it there without you. I *miss* you!"

"I thought you hated me, Richard Stuart, especially after what I overheard you say to my grandfather in the library that day."

He smiled faintly. "I thought *you* hated me then, and I also thought you were in love with Mark Talbot. Besides, this particular Scot does his own courting in his own time, not at anyone else's bidding—not even if that someone is Sir Adam. I would not have come near you then, Janine, and risk the undoubted rebuff which awaited me."

"And now?"

"Now I must risk that rebuff or I will lose you forever. I miss you because I love you, and it took that evening we dined alone together to make me realize how deeply I feel about you."

She stared at him, hardly daring to believe what he was saying.

He put out a hand to her cheek, and caressed it gently with his thumb. "Are you silent because I've amazed you with my impudence or because I've amazed you by admitting such a thing?"

She put her hand over his suddenly. "Silent because you've said the one thing I've dreamed of hearing you say, the one thing I've *wanted* you to say since that first day I spoke with you in the state room at Calworth. I've been in love with you ever since then."

She still felt that it was a dream as he pulled her into his arms and kissed her, that in a moment she would awake and the happiness would dissolve with the morning light. But as he held her, kissing her again, his lips more urgent, she knew that it was no dream; that he loved her—

"It isn't a dream, is it?" she said, her voice muffled against his shoulder. "I'm not going to wake up in a moment?"

"No, it's no dream, I'm here, and I'm going to take you back to Calworth—where you belong. Where we both belong."

His lips were warm and urgent as he kissed her, and she knew then that this was no fantasy; it was real, Richard Stuart was hers.

About the Author

Sandra Heath was born in 1944. As the daughter of an officer in the Royal Air Force, most of her life was spent traveling around to various European posts. She has lived and worked in both Holland and Germany.

The author now resides in Gloucester, England, together with her husband and young daughter, where all her spare time is spent writing. She is especially fond of exotic felines, and at one time or another, has owned each breed of cat.